Captain James Hook and
The CURSE of
Peter Pan

JEREMIAH KLECKNER
JEREMY MARSHALL

Jeremy Marshal: To my mother and father for always supporting me. To my wife who I love. To my sister who believed, I know you made it more than halfway to heaven.

Jeremiah Kleckner: To Avalina, Melissa, and the family and friends who made this possible, thank you for being my inspiration and support.

Because those who can, teach.

Dawn

Chapter One

The tall masts of the dark ship cut deep gashes into the horizon. The flag of Great Britain waves proudly above her sails. Its bold and vivid colors mock the black sheet that is draped over her bow, on which a bleached skull snickers over two crossed bones.

Admiral Charles Price strides to the rail of his flagship, the *Triumph*, to get a better look at the approaching vessel. He watches with steady, unmoving eyes while his men mutter rumors of her cargo, her intent, and her crew. They guess at everything except her name. That fact is known by every man aboard even though no one speaks the words aloud.

Black clouds scheme on the horizon. From the crow's-nest, the lookout shouts down that Royal Navy crewmen are aboard the vessel, waving as they approach. As the ship draws nearer, Admiral Price sees a single man shackled on the deck of the ship. His vivid red coat shines like a beacon against the darkening sky.

"Prepare to board," Admiral Price tells the captain. He

orders his ship alongside the smaller brigantine and watches his crew fall into their stations. Each man knows his place and fulfills his duties without question. There is no wasted movement and no wasted thought. Before long, the crew secures the dark ship and brings her prisoner aboard.

Captain Hook, and his ship, the *Jolly Roger*, have been captured.

A distant thunder rumbles as James Hook stands shackled aboard the British cruiser. His eyes are so narrow that they never seem to blink beneath the dark brush of brow or long curly tendrils of hair.

The silence between the admiral and his captive matures and gives birth to new worries. "Now that he has Captain Hook," the crew mutters, "what will Admiral Price do with a man who has trained under, terrified, or tortured every known pirate in the Caribbean?" Uncertainty grows between both crews as seconds of tension become minutes of anxiety.

"To the brig," the admiral breathes. With the veil of silence pierced, uproarious cheers from both crews nearly shake the boards loose.

Captain Hook smiles with everything but his eyes. Two crewmen take him below deck to the brig. Without a glance back toward his escort, Hook strides through the cell door. He then turns about and seats himself in the center of the bench, legs crossed and arms folded in his lap as one would sit on a gazebo awaiting his Sunday brunch.

His wait is short, however, as Admiral Price slams his heels down on the steps toward the cell door. The two crewmen who first brought Hook aboard now stand guard on either side of the stairway. They part and stiffen at attention as the admiral descends toward them.

Admiral Price motions to the older crewman, hair graying slightly, to get him a chair. The admiral places it alongside a table facing Hook while the much larger crewman brings a parchment scroll and quill.

"The great Captain Hook stands humbled and defeated," Admiral Price says after several long minutes. His voice resounds like gunfire after such a long pause.

"Where I went to school," Hook parries, "this was called sitting." The admiral's jaw clenches, revealing new wrinkles on his already weathered features. His quill falls to the floor and tumbles as if to hide behind his chair. He looks to it, then over to the older crewman, who fetches it seconds too slowly. "If I were to stand," Hook continues, "I would stand in appreciation of British adherence to procedure."

"You'll soon feel the appreciation of a noose," Admiral Price says as his quill scratches the parchment, "Which is why I'm chronicling your final thoughts."

"Is this a personal or professional interest?" Hook asks. Admiral Price looks up for a moment and considers the question.

"A bit of both," he answers. "It is a morbid interest of mine to record the events of the sordid lives of sea criminals. In addition, the records will serve to better train the King's Navy against future assaults."

The larger crewman ducks through the doorway with a tray of tea and biscuits. The admiral motions for him to bring it over and quietly scolds the older crewman for not moving more quickly to set the table.

"And if I say nothing?" Hook asks. He shifts his weight to the other side and swings his right leg over his left. "What then?"

Admiral Price grinds his teeth at the question. His knuckles go white as he clasps the corner of the table before he finally loosens his grip.

"Even in your silence, I will observe your actions and add it to my findings," the admiral says. "You will atone for what you have done."

"And what have I done, Admiral?" Captain Hook asks after a moment of thought.

"The crewmen that brought you aboard informed me that just days ago, you attacked a battleship and managed to kill her captain and all the officers," the admiral says. "The ship sank, but you were overwhelmed by the brave Ensigns and Lieutenants. As the sole surviving pirate, you were taken prisoner on board your own dirty little ship. For that, alone, you will hang. What I am offering you is a chance to make your peace with God before your time."

"And how much time is that exactly?" Hook asks. He flicks open an ornate gold watch in his right hand, glances at it quickly, then deftly places it back into his coat pocket. Its loud ticking is still present, but muffled in the folds of the fabric.

"We are three days from Port Royal," Admiral Price answers. "You will stand trial and most likely be hanged on the morning of the fourth day."

"Port Royal," Hook scoffs. "There is nothing left there for me."

"Well, they have every interest in your return. I have hunted you on their behalf for the better part of a decade," Admiral Price says, "ever since the incident."

"I am honored at the selfless attention you have given me over the years, Admiral," Hook smirks. "Still, how do you know it was me? I've made no such claim."

Admiral Price motions to the larger crewman, who places an

object on the table wrapped in a velvet cloth. The admiral waves the crewman away and peals the cloth back in two quick movements, revealing a flawless steel boarding hook. "Call it a hunch."

"And my ship?" Hook asks.

"As of now, the *Jolly Roger* is needed to accommodate both crews," Price says. "She will be taken back to be studied and dismantled. If you cooperate, I'll spare you the indignity of seeing her stripped by hanging you first."

"How very kind of you," Hook says. "And how far back do you wish for me to go in these tales?"

"A change of heart?" Admiral Price asks. His quill scrapes the paper once again. The distaste of being spoken to so brashly wears off in favor of dreams of promotion and published volumes.

"What harm is it for captured prey to entertain its killer?" Captain Hook responds after checking his watch a second time, bringing the loud tick to a brief crescendo. "Prey is still prey regardless of method. If there is a game to be played between now and the predator's final stroke, I am glad to accept."

The admiral pauses for a small eternity. He finally says that, for the sake of historical accuracy, he would like to know everything.

"Well," Hook shifts his weight again, "if it is, after all, for history's sake, Admiral Price, we do seem to have nothing but time. As with all stories about a man, this one begins with a curious little boy..."

The Tale of a Boy

Chapter Two

The clearest memory of my childhood is the moment it ended.

It was the eve of my thirteenth birthday and I was asleep, as all good children were at that time of night. The shades were pulled back and the window was open to allow a summer's breeze to waft in from the shore. The streets of Port Royal pulsed beneath my window. As the Caribbean stronghold of the Royal Navy, the city was always bustling, but my mother tucked me in hours ago and no common noise could undo her handiwork.

Her stories put the classic authors to shame. She had such a way with words that I wondered if she spoke from experience or from her brilliant imagination. Every night was a new tale of adventure, horror, and heroes. She left me safely tucked away in my bed, protected by a goodnight kiss on my forehead, keeping me safe from all the evil things in life such as trolls, demons, and pirates.

But that didn't deter the visitor. He journeyed from

window to window, peeking in to see what wonders there were to be seen. It is impossible to say what drew him to my house. Whatever the reason may be, the curious boy made it up to the second floor.

In the center of the room was a replica of the naval vessel my father captained. I built it during his time away at sea and encased it in a glass bottle for protection. When he came home, I greeted him with it at the dock. It was the first and last time I saw authentic pride on his face.

The boy poked his head in through the curtains before coming in. It isn't the movement that did it or the scuffling of footfalls, as even now I can't recall whether his feet ever touched the floor.

What woke me was a ruckus that was impossible to ignore. An argument of whispers was followed by a gasp, then the shattering of glass.

I exploded upright, recalling my father's stories about waking to cannon fire. Something breathed near me and I grabbed onto a wrist. My clench tightened out of panic and I screamed. Tears of fright welled up and streamed down the sides of my face. The visitor pulled against my grasp and I was stung with a blinding flash.

My body thumped to the floor beside my bed. My first instinct was to hide beneath it, fearing trolls or demons, but I decided against hiding and scrambled to one knee. I peaked over the side of my bed, searching for whoever attacked me, but saw nothing except an empty room in the dim moonlight.

I did, however, see the first of many tragedies my visitor leaves in the wake of his foolishness. My ship, the replica of my father's vessel, lay broken in the center of my room. The mast was snapped in half and the damage to the hull listed the boat forward and to the left. My heart did the same. I dropped to the floor and began picking up the pieces of that perfect ship.

Then something extraordinary happened. A light swirled and swept about my room, not bound to any candle or lantern. It was a light without heat or fuel. It settled on my desk and I found myself walking toward it as if pulled by an invisible rope. The light was like that of a firework sparkler my father once brought back from a voyage to the Far East.

As I approached it, the light danced from side to side in small jumps, like a grasshopper too stupid to recognize if it is in danger but still trying to keep its distance. The thought gave me an idea, but as I grabbed for an empty jar on my shelf, the light took off and began circling the room again, this time too high to catch.

It was then that I saw the curious boy, perched in the upper corner against the ceiling of my room. That delicate light rushed past his face, igniting his eyes in a terrifying reflection. I screamed again and dropped the jar, causing it to shatter on the floor as well.

"Shh! We don't want any adults to come," the boy said. "They will ruin all the fun we can have. My name is Peter Pan. I saw the ship through the window and wanted to play with it. I love playing captain and don't have any toys that look that nice where I'm from."

"I am James Hoodkins," I told him, wiping a tear from my cheek. I rose from the ruin of my broken ship to meet him eye to eye. "And there are more polite ways to ask if someone wants to play than bursting into their room at night." He nodded as if trying to understand.

"Why are you crying?" he asked.

"I wasn't crying."

"Yes, you were. Just before."

I told him that having tears of shock are not the same thing as crying. Although I had never been more terrified of any man or creature in my short life, I was surely not going to show such poor form by giving him that satisfaction.

"You wrecked my ship," I told him, pointing to the mess on the floor.

"That was her fault," he said. The light began to furiously encircle his head, creating a sort of halo. He argued with it, as a crazy person would talk to himself in the night. The glow of the argument lit up his blonde hair and dirty green outfit. When he began to float down from the ceiling, the boy and his light stopped squabbling.

"How do you do that?" I asked.

The boy stared blankly at me and asked, "Do what?"

"Come now," I said. "Don't be silly. How do you fly like that?" The boy laughed as he glided around the room, twirling and spinning.

"I think a happy thought," he said. "Then I take to the air and I'm off to my next big adventure." He soared for several more moments before asking, "Well, James Hoodkins, what do you want to play?" Hundreds of answers raced through my mind, but only one idea interested me.

"I want to fly."

Peter's eyes filled up with joy and he was once again in the air.

"Just think of a happy thought and let it lift you away." Of the joys that flooded to mind, my Emily's love conquered all. With my eyes closed, I leapt, expecting to take flight among angels. I hung in the air for an instant and then fell to the floor with a thud.

"What happened?" I asked, looking up at Peter with betrayal in my eyes. "That was the happiest thought I had." His face wrinkled with confusion. After a moment, he snapped his fingers and smiled.

"That's right, you need fairy dust as well."

"And you didn't think that was important enough to tell me before? I could have leapt to my death out of the window."

"But you didn't," Pan said. He placed his hands on his hips as if to stress how proud he was of his keen observation.

"Well," I started, trying to sound less angry than I was, "Where can I get fairy dust?"

"Where else?" Pan laughed. He pointed over to the corner of my room where the sparkling light rested on the lid of a trunk of old toys.

"Her name is Tinkerbell," Peter said. I nodded to it politely. "She's a fairy."

"Rubbish," I said on reflex. A flying boy was one thing, but a fairy was too far beyond belief. Yet, the instant that the word came out of my mouth, the light went out and the creature hurdled to the floor. Peter dashed through the air, caught it, and brought it to my desk in a rush.

"You've killed her," he said. A sob brewed beneath his words.

"Now we've each destroyed something the other cherishes," I said, not really meaning it but still hurt from the loss of my replica ship and the fall to the floor. "We're even." I turned my back to the scene, but softened at the sound of tears. I had so few visitors, day or night, due to my condition. I shouldn't make a habit of sending new friends away, even ones as odd as this unnatural child and his sparkler.

What I saw when I walked over to him mocked the barrier between what was and what shouldn't be. The doused light was in fact a small woman, no bigger than a child's thumb, with the wings of an insect. She, too, was dressed like Peter, in a sort of green vegetation woven into tattered cloth.

"You can save her," Peter said, choking back tears. "You have to say that you believe in fairies."

"I don't know if I can," I told him. "This is like some dream."

"You have to say it!"

If she were still just a light, it would have been easy to doubt her existence. As I stood over her wilted little body, my conviction melted at the edges. The walls of my truth collapsed with thundering silence as a whole world of possibilities opened up to me. She undeniably existed and she was undeniably dying.

"I do believe in fairies," I said. A spark burst from her mouth. I repeated it and more sparks flew. I said it a third time and the light exploded around her, lifting her up. He leapt to meet her and I watched as they circled my room in celebration.

"Is she alright?" I asked. My words stopped Peter and the light cold. He bent over and whispered to Tinkerbell. She responded, but no matter how hard I listened, I could only hear the ringing and chiming of little bells. I stepped closer to better hear her unusual noises.

"What's she saying?" I asked. "I don't understand her."

"That's just how they talk," Peter explained.

"Does she still have enough fairy dust to help me fly, too?" I asked. She continued ringing and he began to laugh.

"She says 'no' because you're an ugly boy and you wouldn't know a fairy if it flew in and poked you on the nose," he giggled.

"She's a vile little thing, isn't she?" This time Tinkerbell darted right up to my face and rang loudly. Having been raised by a British Captain and knowing sailors my whole life, I could only imagine what she was saying now.

"It's not her fault," Pan said. "Fairies are so small that they can only feel or think one thing at a time. Right now, she hates you because you killed her." I turned back to Tinkerbell in time to see her give me the most obscene gesture before she soared through the open window into the night's sky.

"That wasn't very adult of her," I said, a little insulted.

"Adults," Peter said under his breath. "All they want us to do is grow up."

"We all must grow up sometime, Peter."

"Not me," he laughed. "I'll be a boy forever."

The word "rubbish" formed on my lips, but I caught myself before it was spoken. Memories of the last time I jumped to judgment rushed through my mind. I could no longer afford the comfort of growing comfortable in my truths.

"I have to go after Tink," Peter said as he glided over to the window. "In the mood she's in, she can get into all sorts of trouble." He smirked at me as if to hint at yet grander secrets.

"Are you coming back?" I asked. He puzzled over the question for long moments before finally answering.

"I don't know."

Peter leapt through the window and was gone in an instant. He left me standing in the mess of a broken ship and shattered glass, but I didn't mind. Pan made anything possible and I wanted to know all of it.

Chapter Three

The next morning I stormed down the stairs, the thunder of my footfalls shook the house around me. While cleaning my room last night, I pieced together a thousand ways to tell my mother about the strange boy who flew into my room. She was a believer. She must have seen them, or something like them, before. My mind raced with wonder at what adventures she could share now that I believed as she did.

I leapt down the final four steps and raced to the dining room. I burst through the door crying out, "Mother! Mother, your stories are true! Peter Pan can fly!"

But it wasn't my mother's warm laugh that greeted me first. The cold stare of my father stopped me as dead as gunfire. He sat at the head of the table in full uniform, his face reddening slightly.

"Father," I breathed. "You're back days early." He said nothing. Instead, he nodded at one of the place settings and drew his lips tighter at the corners, instructing me to sit and remain silent. Father's magic was different than my mother's in that he could express whole ideas with simple looks.

As I moved to the table, I noticed the fourth place setting. A hand clasped down on my shoulder before I had a chance to ask who the setting was for.

"Your father and I were carried away on slightly different business," a voice said just behind my ear. It was barely above a whisper, but I knew it well. I looked up at a man with lean, sharp features and steel-gray eyes.

"Mr. Ashley," my father said, "come and sit with us."

"I'd be delighted," Mr. Ashley responded. Heath Ashley served under my father since he first entered the Royal Navy. Father always spoke highly of him and, whenever Father was home, Heath Ashley was always at the house performing one task or another. Only in the last year did Heath receive a commission to serve as a first officer on a different vessel. We hadn't seen much of him since then.

We were already seated when Mother came in from the kitchen, carrying trays of food.

"Well, I for one am thrilled that you are home," she said as she took her place at Father's side. We rose and stood until she was seated, like gentlemen of good form should.

"You look exhausted, Heath. What have you been doing?" Mother asked.

"I've been searching for the missing boy all night," he responded. "Dr. Sotheby's kid."

"That's dreadful," Mother said. "James, you remember Donald Sotheby from school, the one with the curly hair?" I nodded and recalled that the last time I saw him. He and one of the other boys got into a scrap on the way home. Curly always liked playing jokes on other kids and it must have caught up to him that time.

"So, how is your commission?" Mother asked Heath after a long pause.

"It has held many surprises," he said, "and many rewards." Father's eyes widened and tensed at the edges. It was not uncommon to hear them go on for hours about the most trivial details of life at sea. This hush between them unsettled me.

"Rewards?" Mother asked. She darted a questioning look between Heath and my father.

"Heath is getting his own command," Father said. "By this time next month, he'll be the youngest captain in the fleet."

"That's outstanding," Mother applauded as her face alighted with joy. "Which ship will you have?"

"The *Champlain*," Heath responded.

"Isn't that the ship you are already on?" I asked.

"Indeed," Heath said. "The captain I am serving under is being promoted to admiral." Mother gave Father a puzzled look but didn't speak. Confused, I said what she was thinking.

"But, Father, weren't you supposed to be promoted to admiral after this last voyage?" All three turned to me, but I wasn't sure why. It was a perfectly fine question.

"It seems that Heath knew which man to back in this fight," Father said.

"You did the right thing stepping aside this time, John," Heath said. "The King's Navy will have an Admiral Hoodkins soon enough. Besides, as I recall we both followed his lead on this last, most worthwhile venture." Father tensed again and fixed his eyes firmly on Ashley.

"What about you, James?" Heath asked me without once looking in my direction. "You seemed quite excited when you first came down stairs."

"What do you mean?" Mother asked, happy to change the subject.

"Oh, you missed it," Heath continued with a laugh. "James came running down the stairs shouting 'You were right, Mother! Your stories are true!' It was a sight."

"I don't know if this is the right time to talk of bedtime stories, Heath," Mother said with a cautious look.

"Nonsense," he insisted. "Who doesn't want to hear of dangerous adventures and hidden treasure?"

"It's not important now," I said. There was no part of my father that wanted to hear about flying boys and I was sure that Heath was equally as disinterested in fairies.

"It seemed of dire importance a few minutes ago," Heath said. "Tell me, who is this Peter Pan?"

"He's just some boy," I told him.

"Who flies?" Heath goaded.

"Yes, sir," I responded after some time. I tried to hold it back, but the words kept coming. "He came into my room last night while I was sleeping. I wouldn't have heard him if he didn't wreck the ship I'd built." Father's face reddened, then cooled as solid as tempered steel. "He and Tinkerbell..."

"Who?" Heath asked, amused.

"His fairy friend," I responded. "Tinkerbell died because I said I didn't believe in fairies." Mother gasped and turned whiter than the linen. Heath let out a bellow while my father just sat there and wrinkled his brow. "But don't worry, I said that I did believe and she came back to life."

"Naturally," Heath added. Mother gave me a worried smile. Her smiles were usually so inviting, the type that let you know everything would be just fine. This one was different. In fact, the only one who seemed to enjoy the tale was Heath Ashley. His smile was pulled tight across his teeth. It would have been warm if not for the coldness of his eyes.

"Enough," Father said.

"Oh, John," Heath said, "let the boy speak. The fairy did survive, after all."

"Enough!" Father yelled and slammed his fist against the table. The silence grew to cover the whole room until only the clocks dared to tick onward. If not for their measured beats, I would have sworn that all time had stopped.

"Perhaps I should be going," Heath said. Father met his eyes with a look of shame and rage. Heath Ashley strode toward the door, but turned before he left. "Don't give up on your imagination, James. It'll make you an amazing scholar, now that your father can afford it."

We finished our food in silence. Even though I was not sure what I did wrong, I knew that I should not make matters worse. Considering that I had not had many visitors because of my condition, especially other children my own age, I expected my parents to be elated at the news that I made a new friend. The doctors believed that my fatigue and spells of dizziness were due to my blood's unusual thickness and color. Wounds healed well but I had to be wary not to push myself to the point of exhaustion, which came quickly. As a result, I spent days at a time letting and gathering my strength.

"Solitude and staying indoors is unhealthy for a boy of your breeding and intention," Father said, shattering the uneasy quiet. This was the start of the usual argument. Mother was gentler regarding my condition and rushed to my aid. When discussion was permitted on the subject, she spoke on behalf of tutors and visitation. She didn't wait for permission to speak this time. She, like I, heard a tone of inevitability in Father's voice.

"The boy is ill," she began. "He needs to stay home to rest."

"The boy should only rest for as long as is immediately necessary and attend school like a gentleman," Father said while waving his hand as if he were batting her words away.

"After this next voyage, I'll be promoted to admiral," he began. "We'll return to England. I have already registered James at Eton. He will go this fall and be the scholar we have prepared him to be." Mother stood beside me and pressed my head against her hip. I tried to make myself smaller than that fairy. My failure to disappear was clear when I saw my father examine me.

"But first, he needs hardening," he said. "I have room for two cabin boys." My mother gasped. "He can let on the ship when necessary. There is little running, the work is methodical in pace, and he can study on board."

At that, the conversation was over. Father continued to talk, but it was only of how this would unfold, not whether it would. He drafted two letters. One went to my school, the other to his first mate, Mr. Jukes. Mother wept and clasped an old cloth.

My confusion led to anger. My blood boiled and I bolted through the door. Of all the places in the world, there was only one that brought any comfort to me aside from my room. It was a place that only one other knew about. I had to see Emily. She alone would understand and she alone would know where to find me. She would be there as soon as news of my flight reached her.

Chapter Four

My feet pounded the cobblestone for only brief moments. Soon, the soft earth padded my footfalls. There was a lagoon not far from town, that part was no secret. People knew of it, but rarely visited as they were often busy with the responsibilities of maintaining the port. Sometimes swimmers played in the cool glassy water.

Our spot was just above the lagoon. Cut into the cove was a cliff with a steep drop off into the water. If you squinted, the pale colors of the lagoon that danced in the moonlight were also ablaze in the setting or rising sun. There was no wrong time of day to be there as it was rife with infinite moments of perfection.

She knew I'd be there. It was our secret place, away from parents and responsibilities. We knew every hidden rock in the tall grass and every soft patch of dirt, where your foot sinks unexpectedly deep. It was the one place where getting older doesn't mean growing up.

My anger took me again. I kicked rocks and beat the earth

with my fists. I ground my heel against the trees and scraped moss with bark. I did everything but cry. I am unsure how long her slight frame stood watching me. It didn't matter.

Emily had seen me in every state of being, from my proudest crowing to my most boiling rage. In every instance, she spoke to the matter afflicting me, not my reaction to it. She knew of my condition and visited me, often bringing my daily assignments from classes that I missed. She was always cool, never cold. As the golden-haired daughter of Harrison Jukes, Father's first officer and longtime friend, it was assumed that we were to be married when the time suited us. It was the one thing that was planned for me to which I had no objection.

She came to where I was kneeling and placed a still hand on my shoulder, saying nothing. The thick blood in my veins slowed its pounding in my ears enough for me to hear a breeze kiss each leaf, calming me further. Soon, I was calm enough to pull thoughts together and tether them with reason.

"You came," I said as my first attempt at civilized conversation. It was meant to sound like a question, but I knew better than to have doubts.

"You didn't think I would?"

"It's not that, I just didn't think you'd make it here so quickly," I told her, still clearing the fog of rage from my head.

"Billy told me," she said. Emily's brother, William, was two years my junior, but healthy and broad of shoulder like Mr. Jukes. Father was often entertained and slightly envious of the tales his first mate would tell of William's minor disasters. "He heard it from Thomas Darling out in the shipyard. He said that you ran off when you heard that Donald Sotheby went missing."

"Well, Thomas Darling shouldn't run his mouth without

knowing the whole story," I said, a little annoyed. "Something amazing happened."

We lay on the rocks overlooking the lagoon as I detailed last night's adventure with the flying boy and his fairy. I explained my father's decision and my mother's tears and her clasping of the old cloth. I told her everything. The whole time, she looked up at the sky and said nothing. While she listened, her face twisted from compassion mixed with loss to one of knowing acceptance.

"We knew that you would eventually go off to sea like our fathers," she said.

"Just not so soon," I answered, only now becoming aware that she had prepared for this moment far more thoroughly than I had. She said nothing of what I told her about Peter. Whether she believed me or would later investigate my condition to learn if it caused hallucinations, I was certain that she would discuss it with no one. It was at this moment that I resolved not to discuss Pan with anyone else until I could prove that he was real or be sure the secret of our meeting would be kept.

"Still, there is an advantage to you going this time," she said after a long pause. The words stung me with surprise. The wound was surely visible as she followed with the explanation. "The other cabin boy is going to be my brother, Billy."

It seemed that my father and Mr. Jukes made the decision some time ago that their two sons would serve with them as cabin boys in an effort to develop us into fine sailors and future officers. The story of Peter Pan was Father's breaking point. The letter he wrote to Harrison Jukes tied William's fate to mine.

"You need to promise me that no harm will come to him, James." She raised her emerald eyes to meet mine, knowing that I couldn't refuse her while they were upon me. I wondered whether she had already had this same conversation with William, making him watch over me as well. It was a brilliant maneuver and I admired her for it.

"Of course," I said. I swore to it in her name. She knew I could be held to my word. It is poor form to go back on an oath and I am nothing if not a gentleman.

Chapter Five

The weeks melted into one another as the day of my departure approached. Mother took this opportunity to spend as much time in my room as possible. Every few minutes she found some excuse to polish or straighten something. I didn't mind her attention.

The night before I was to ship out under my father's command, she sat alongside my bed and told me her last story. There was something different, however, something wrong. Usually, her eyes spark ever so slightly before she begins, but that night she seemed lost, as if looking for a path in a dark wood. I decided to light one for her.

"Can I hear about knights and monsters one last time?" I asked her. She looked at me and the spark lit up her sad eyes.

"Stories about monsters are easy in this world," she sighed.

"I knew it," I burst. "I knew you believed. We don't have to tell Father about it though. He wouldn't understand."

"Your father knows about monsters all too well, I'm afraid. He sees them every time he steps onto that ship."

"Pirates," I told her. Father was a renowned pirate-hunter and I'd heard his adventures many times before. Father, Harrison Jukes, and Heath Ashley often sat around the fireplace and terrified us with tales of firefights and narrow escapes. These were the men who lived it, as I would soon, but they were not storytellers. Somehow their adventures paled before Mother's retellings.

"Three years ago," she leaned in, "your father chased down the dread pirate Henry Davis to a small island off the coast of Jamaica." She went on to tell of how Father didn't fire until after he offered the vermin a chance for a peaceful surrender. They answered with cannon fire and Father returned in kind.

Mother rocked from side to side, recounting each shot, and covered me in my bed to protect me from the spray of kindling from the impacts. She told of how the pirates scurried to their lifeboats and made for the nearest shore. Heath led the first wave in pursuit, carrying the battle to them on land. Father and Harrison Jukes came shortly after, quickly overpowering the pirates and saving young Ashley from Davis's sword.

She continued to brilliantly act out each scene of the battle. She hacked and slashed the air, using her old cloth as a sword. Yet, even as she played out the daring adventure, I could only think of the last time Heath Ashley was over the house and how he repaid my father for his generosity and guidance.

"Why did Heath not support Father?" I asked, cutting her performance short. She stopped mid-swipe and turned to meet my eyes with a cautious look. "Father took him in, trained him, even saved his life and for what? What about Mr. Jukes? He should have been considered for command before Heath."

"Mr. Jukes is a loyal first officer," she explained, "and Heath wanted to captain his own ship. Once his captain was promoted to admiral, then the command of the *Champlain* opened for him to take."

"But that's so ungrateful," I told her.

"James, you can teach a man to do the right thing, but that doesn't mean that his heart is good. Men can be more evil than any myth and they can do it without the help of magic or enchantments. Your father knows this and it helps give him strength. No matter what evil makes a man act as he does, your father knows that whatever he faces is only a man, nothing more."

Just like any other night, she placed a kiss on my forehead, but not to protect me from demons, trolls, or dragons. No, this kiss was to protect me from the very real evils of this world that she and my father knew all too well.

"Your father and I love you very much, James," she said before blowing out the candle and locking my bedroom window.

Chapter Six

Shattered glass sprayed my room in the gathering light of early dawn. This time, I was not shocked by it. In fact, it was a welcome sound, one that I'd hoped to hear before the morning of my departure arrived. I flew from my bed, ready to take off into the horizon.

"Peter!" I shouted as I peered out the fist-sized hole in the pane. "Where are you?" Moments of elation were swallowed by doubt and concern. Then, a face swung down from above the window, but not the face I expected.

"Can you let me in?" William asked. Stunned, I fell back onto the glass-covered floor. William climbed down to the ledge of the window and smirked as he gently tapped the frame. "I don't have any more rocks."

"What are you doing here, William?" I asked as I brushed myself off and unlatched the window. William tumbled in, his feet landing heavily on the floor. He was taller than I last saw him, inches taller than I was and far heavier. I looked down at the shattered glass at my feet and then met his eyes. He nodded and we both began picking up the pieces.

"I just came by to make sure that you picked up your books."

"And who sent you?" I asked. The question caught him off his guard and he froze for a few seconds.

"Captain Hoodkins," he said.

"What? Father didn't think I'd get my schoolwork?"

"No, he just didn't want me to carry them for you this time," William said. Father seemed more determined than ever to harden me into adulthood.

William was not as witty or insightful as his sister, Emily, but he did have a singular talent. On command, he could come up with a quartet for whatever he was doing at the time. He started this working song in low tones at first.

> "The sparkling glass of window pane,
> Sullies your pristine floor.
> We stoop down now to pick it up,
> And soon there'll be no more."

"Why didn't you just use the door?" I asked him when our chorus was over.

"Who wants to use doors when you can climb buildings?" he asked in return. "You don't want to climb down with me? It's fun."

"I'll meet you out front," I told him. William bounded through the window and scaled down the side of the house with ease, but before dashing off on his way to the front door he turned and asked about something I'd hoped he'd not heard, "One last thing, James. Who's Peter?"

"No one," I lied. "Just a dream."

Emily helped William and me carry our books and study supplies home. A list of our assignments was written on parchment and rolled into scrolls, one for each course. At first, Father marveled at the amount of school work we were given for the short voyage, but I assured him that we would finish it before we got back as long as we were given a few hours a day.

"Time is very important," he said, flicking open his grandfather's gold watch. "You can never escape your studies. If you fail to do them, time will eventually catch up to you." He glanced down at the watch in his right hand and then snapped it shut and looked up as if to say "It's time to go."

The goodbye I shared with my mother was short.

"I'm sorry," I told her. "When I return I will be the man that you always wanted me to be." She leaned down with tears on her cheeks and held me.

"I couldn't ask for a better son," she said. "I know you will make me proud because you have already done so time and time again." She told me to be careful and to keep safe, all the while looking at my father. Our last hug was the one I used to bring myself to sleep each night for months after. I closed the door to my house, saying goodbye to all childish things, and walked toward adulthood.

The *Britannia* was just as I had rebuilt her as a model. She was a tall, older brigantine. I knew every inch of that deck. I used plans to build the model, but never saw the inside until that day. The kitchen, the galley, crew quarters, I'd only seen them in my mind. After this voyage the ship is to be decommissioned and knowing that made this moment all the sweeter.

The greatest treasure was standing in the captain's quarters.

However modest by current engineering standards, it was still by far the grandest room I had ever laid eyes upon. On Father's desk were a stack of charts. The lines of degrees and courses plotted fascinated me. Pan could fly, but the gift of mathematics was mine. Within seconds I memorized our location and route.

"Don't touch anything," Father snapped. "My cabin is not for play. Only serious work goes on here." Somehow, his scolding made the room more appealing than ever.

At that moment, First Officer Jukes stepped into the cabin. He ducked through the frame and stood at attention. William and Emily scurried behind him. William was covered in bruises and dirt as if he'd already fought in the darkest parts of Africa before waking this morning. Emily was pristine, but not above rapping William and me on the nose with our literature scrolls.

The room chilled suddenly and I felt the hairs on my neck bristle. As one, we turned to the doorway and were stopped cold by a man with sharp features in a captain's uniform. His eyes were gray and dead. The pain that it took for him to smile must have been unbearable, but he managed it.

"Captain Ashley," my father called out in an even tone, "You know James already."

"Indeed I do," Heath said, pulling his strained smile further across his face to show teeth.

"James will be joining me on this trip," Father added, "and maybe more."

"Well, I can't think of a better teacher than your father," Captain Ashley said. "He taught me everything I know about sailing." I nodded slowly but didn't find words that weren't barbed with venom. His demeanor visibly stiffened as his frustration with me grew. He turned his eyes to the other children.

"William. Emily. You remember Heath Ashley, don't you?" Father said. "He's a captain now. His ship is departing a day after ours." They greeted him like a young lady and gentleman should.

"Are we all coming along this time?" Captain Ashley said. Heath looked over William, but observed Emily more closely.

"No, sir," she told him. She met his eyes for an instant before turning her gaze to the floor. William answered as well, but his words were lost on Captain Ashley, whose face was a mixture of promise and disappointment.

"Well," he said, "then I look forward to seeing you upon my return." He had the look of a man whose pig was still too thin to slaughter. It was at that moment that I decided to hate the man. I seethed beneath my skin and was only stopped from action by Mr. Jukes, who placed one hulking hand over Captain Ashley's shoulder.

"Maybe," he suggested, "the children should go and get more familiar with the ship?"

"Indeed," Captain Ashley exhaled. My father excused William, Emily, and me from the cabin so that he and the other men could discuss business.

William refused to stop talking, so we lost him behind the main deck. There, I was a thief for the first time. Emily said that she kissed me for luck, but I knew that I stole it fair and square.

Chapter Seven

The days aboard my father's ship, the *Britannia*, were difficult for me. Father didn't like the idea of favoritism, which explained the grueling nature of the job. William was assigned to my father and I was assigned to his. I heard about the training of Mr. Jukes from Father's late night stories. He was considered one of the toughest men in the Royal Navy with good reason. I found out why on the first day.

After swabbing the deck for the third time, I reported to Mr. Jukes. He was talking with the navigator but stopped briefly to glance over his shoulder.

"Do it again," he said before turning his attention back to Mr. Stevenson.

"Aren't you even going to look?" I asked. The request visibly stunned the much larger man. The men chuckled to themselves as he adjusted his herculean frame. A mere look from his fist-sized eyes silenced them.

"I said 'Do it again', Mr. Hoodkins," he bellowed. Furious

and tired I told him of my condition. He nodded as if he understood, but then said, "One good job can easily take the place of four poor ones." I began to mouth another complaint, but he cut through my words with dizzying speed.

"Take pride in your work and no words will be necessary," he told me. "Your work must speak on your behalf."

"I'd like to talk to my father," I told him.

"Your father?" Mr. Jukes laughed. "You lost your father the moment you stepped on this ship. The captain does his rounds at noon, and no sooner. Your work had best be done by then." With that, Mr. Jukes left me to my tasks.

When William and I were not running messages between the officers, we were doing one dirty task or another. We cleaned the clothing, prepared the food for cooking, hitched the sheets, and learned how to powder the cannons during battle. Although it was hard work, we took pride in keeping our fathers happy.

Mr. Jukes even took the time to teach me knot-tying and sword-fighting. I mastered knots in days as each could be expressed in mathematical terms. Sword-fighting was more of a challenge. As I was not strong enough to block most attacks, he taught me to evade and disarm. The short, quick movements were easy enough to remember, but I tired too quickly to last in a prolonged battle.

Having been kept home so long due to my condition, my muscles weren't hard enough for this type of work. William adapted more quickly, easily outpacing me in our physical duties.

In the evenings, we lay on the floor of the captain's quarters and attacked our studies. This was where I more than repaid William for any help with the physical work earlier in the day. My mathematics assignments were done within three days. Out of boredom, I did Williams' in such a way so that he could study from them without getting any answers. It would be poor form to cheat.

Literature takes longer, but not because it was difficult. One book, in particular, held my interest and took several reads to fully absorb. In it, there was a play about two couples that got lost in a forest. They were bewitched through a magic that was controlled by two beings of great power. There were fairies and transmutations and, caught up in the heartbreak and whimsy, there was a short imp named Puck. He was joyful and confident like Pan. There was a mirth about him that brought light to the darkest parts of the story.

When the time for our studies ended, William and I swabbed the deck of the ship. It was our last task before we went to our beds in the crew barracks. Without regular maintenance, the ship could become unfit for proper British use in days.

Weeks into the voyage, we docked at our first port. There was a rumor among the men that there were new orders and that our simple supply run would soon be much more.

We were delighted to be close to the adventure as our fathers took us with them to meet the new admiral. The admiral's headquarters wasn't more than a mile into town and had an amazing view of the port. The men walked ahead of us and I found myself staring off to the open sea before realizing that I was being spoken to.

"James," my father snapped. "The admiral was addressing you."

"It's quite alright, Captain," the admiral said. "He wouldn't be a Hoodkins if he weren't enthralled with the horizon."

My father, Officer Jukes, and the admiral exchanged pleasantries. There was a tone of seriousness to their light conversation that was unsettling. When we finally reached the admiral's office, I saw Captain Ashley through the open door and was reminded what unsettling truly meant. He looked at me with disdain and curled a corner of his mouth into a snicker. The blood rose into my face as my eyes devoured him with hatred.

William and I remained in the hall as the meeting continued. We played for hours but kept the door in view. When it opened, our fathers were changed men. The crew didn't hear the new orders until later, but from that moment forward, the whole tone of the journey changed. There were fewer smiles and far less laughter.

That same night, as usual, William finished his side of the ship first. He went off to bed and I was left on the bow. As I secured the tethers to the forward mast, I was alone with my thoughts. In them, Emily smiled and moved in to kiss me gently. Her lips parted to tell me something that I cannot hear. I closed my eyes and a small voice came from above.

"I saw your ship and want to play with it," the mild voice said. "I don't have any toys that look this nice where I'm from. My name's Peter. Peter Pan."

Chapter Eight

"I'm Peter Pan," the child said proudly. He was standing on the mast as if it were the floorboards of the deck. I had seen him fly before and although this was nothing new, I was still amazed.

"I'm James," I told him. It didn't bother me that I had to reintroduce myself. "We've met before." His blank expression told me of his genuine surprise that we knew each other. "We played weeks ago in my room in Port Royal."

"Oh," was all he said, as if bored already. I decided to retell one of the adventures in my literature books as if it were one of ours.

"Did I say my room?" I led. "I meant we played in a magical forest." His head turned and bent to the side with interest. "You and I had a jolly time robbing wealthy carriages and saving England from the evil prince and his sheriff." His eyes burst with excitement as I retold the whole adventure.

We laughed for a few minutes before I remembered that

telling my parents about my first meeting with Peter got me removed from school and put on this ship. It was that thought that reminded me of the other crewmen on deck. A flying boy would be difficult to explain to the officers.

Pan was an expert in evading grownups. He hid on the side of the ship or behind a mast. He even hid in plain view between barrels and behind sheets. The crewmen just passed by each time, looking at me as if I'd been talking to the wind.

"I have a wonderful idea for a game," Peter said. It's obvious that he had become bored with hiding. He bent to my ear as if his idea were a great secret that no one else could know. "I'll steer the ship and you'll be my first mate."

"We can't do that," I told him. "There are crewmen on watch all night. One of them always steers."

"Oh. I wanted to steer," Peter said. He shrank as if all of the air was squeezed out of him.

"Besides," I said. "The ship is a place of serious work." This news was more disappointing to him than I expected.

"There's no talk about work in Neverland," Peter said.

"Neverland?" I asked. "I've never heard of such a place."

"That's my home," Pan said. He pointed to the sky. "It's easy to get there," he boasted. "You have to find the second star to the right and follow it until morning. However, only one of my cleverness, not to mention my skill, can survive there."

He looked up to the stars for a minute. Then his eyes settled on the door to my father's quarters.

He instantly sprang upright and said, "I don't have to steer to be captain. Steering is for the men to do." He glided on air to the captain's cabin. "I'm so clever."

"No!" I whispered. "Don't go in there! That's my father's

room!"

"You're father is the captain?" Peter said as he opened the door. "Then he won't mind if we use his room for a little while."

I'd been cleaning the opposite side of the ship and didn't know if Father was in his quarters or below deck. Pan was taking a gamble by barging in as he did. My heart leapt as Peter dove through the door into the darkness of the cabin. I looked to make sure that I was not being watched and followed.

"We can't be in here," I said.

"But we are," Peter said. He looked around the room and smiled, proud with himself for winning the argument.

"That's not what I mean, Peter," I said with growing frustration. "We're not supposed to be here."

Pan didn't bother responding. He was too busy digging through my father's trunk. He grabbed a uniform coat and tied it around his neck. He then pulled a short sword from his waistband and swung it wildly about the room.

I ran to him to take my father's things back, careful of his blade. I couldn't let him wreck the whole ship in the name of a good time. Besides, I was sure my father would notice that his uniform was no longer as he left it.

Pan floated upside down above my father's desk and lit a candle. The flickering light danced on the navigator's charts. I didn't see them in the pitch black, but now they shined like the moon on a clear night.

"What are those?" Peter asked, noticing that he was no longer the center of my attention. "They look boring."

"Far from it," I said. "This is the route the navigator, Mr. Stevenson, plotted." Peter looked at me blankly. "These maps show the direction that the ship is going and how it is going to get there."

Pan was already looking around for something else to do, so I picked up my father's sword and told him what the crew learned earlier. "We're going to capture pirates."

"Pirates?" Peter squealed. "What a game that would be." He repeated this several times as he slashed the air with the sword. "What I wouldn't give to fight pirates! Who are we catching?" His next swing came too close and our steel clashed. His eyes flashed with wild excitement. I pushed him back and raised my guard.

"His name is Jesse Labette," I said, dodging a wild swing. "He is a dreadful pirate who steals whatever he can and kills everyone in his way."

"He sounds as bad as the Sheriff we fought the last time we met," Peter said, referring to the story I told him.

"Not exactly, Peter," I corrected. "This time, we're on the side of the law and we're not corrupt." I swung high and thrust low. The sword was heavy in my hands, so he flew between attacks with ease. He's fast and well-practiced. If I could only ground him, I'd at least have a chance at keeping up. "Also, pirates don't usually fight head on. They have smaller ships so that they can sail in shallow water and avoid the bigger British ships."

"Isn't it better if he hides?" Peter asked. "It doesn't seem like much fun if they don't try to hide first."

"I don't think he feels that he has to hide," I said. "The crew tells rumors of a massive cannon on the bow. They call it Long Tom. It's a ship killer." Peter gasped. He then lowered his sword and looked back at my father's desk.

"Those maps still look boring," he said, "and I want to play captain."

The charts called my eyes back to them with each flicker of the candle. I traced my fingers over the course that I memorized the last time I saw them. There were new lines plotted now. One circled around against the current to a gulf on the south side of an island. The other sloped in from the north. The meeting place was marked with a cross. Mr. Stevenson had to be a fool for plotting this trip so carelessly. In seconds, I figured out that the southern course could get to the location much faster sailing with the current and with a more direct route.

Then I got an idea that was far cleverer than Peter's.

"You can," I said. I told him that as captain, he could order me to make a course correction. "This is part of what the captain does."

Pan agreed as long as he was the one giving orders. That was fine by me since I was telling him what orders to give.

Peter flew around the cabin while I was busy at work. Charting a route was easy. I even found the difference in the amount of time and food that was saved by following this course.

I was just putting away my father's things when the door creaked. Peter dove through the window. I ran to the porthole to see him fly into the distance and vanish from sight. The door rattled open. Father didn't see me at first, but when he did, I was too far from his desk to arouse suspicion.

Now was not the time for him to see my skills at work. I told him that my condition made me tired and it would be bad form to let the crew to see me that way. With a nod, he sent me off.

I feigned exhaustion until I was out of his sight. I flew to my bunk and dove under the sheet. In one night, I proved Pan was real, made a fool out of Mr. Stevenson, and left the surprise of a lifetime for father.

Chapter Nine

The ship listed to one side and I was thrown off of my bunk. An argument of whispers was followed by a gasp, then the crash of glass on the hardwood floor. I landed on pieces of a broken lantern. The men ran past and over me. Heavy footfalls muffled what was being said. I pulled the glass from my arms as I made my way on deck. Waiting for me was the island I expected, but with a surprise that I didn't.

Dawn broke over the mast of a ship in the distance. Her dark masts cut deep gashes into the horizon. Smoke billowed from her sides. The shock of the fall still clouded my head. I realized what was happening only after seeing a black flag, its white skull and crossed cutlasses danced in the wind.

Pirates.

My thoughts went to finding William. I made a promise to Emily that I intended to keep. I weaved through the crew as they scrambled to their posts. Like gears in a machine, they worked as one without variation. William was easily found cowering among men. It was a sight that I'd never let him live down. For the first time, I was the one who was strong and fearless.

In battle, William and I had a job to do. I shook him into the moment and we hurried below deck. Along each side of the ship was a row of cannons. The crew had already lined them on the port side. William and I brought the barrels of gunpowder. We returned with the first barrel when we were fired upon again. The ship rocked as we heard wood splintering above deck.

"Long Tom will send us all to a watery grave," Mr. Stevenson cried.

We loaded and packed the gunpowder. The men placed the cannon balls and lit the fuse. Seconds later, thunder sounded.

We immediately began loading and packing again. I noticed that the pirate ship was closer. I tried to make my adjustments to the angle of the cannon look like an accident. Mr. Stevenson swatted me away and aimed the cannon in haste. Thunder sounded and the shot missed for the second time.

Over the hum in my ears, I heard my father shouting orders. Through the hole in the deck I saw his frustration.

"Where's Captain Ashley?" he barked at Mr. Jukes. Heath Ashley. Selfishness was one thing, but this was a betrayal that cannot stand. I swore I'd slay him for it, if for nothing else.

Another two crashes sheared the main deck from the ship and my father was gone.

There was nothing but sky over me now. The salt spray stung my cuts. I stood alone among prone bodies. Three were dead, two were groaning. William stirred but didn't get up.

Everything my father and Mr. Jukes had taught me led to this moment.

The mast snapped in half and the damage to the hull listed

the boat forward and to the left. The pitch of the floor was at twenty-three degrees and rising at the stern. Mr. Stevenson, a man who was useless in life, was now invaluable to me in death as I wedged his body behind the cannon to prevent it from rolling. I righted the upturned barrel and packed the cannon with powder. The ball was heavy with potential.

Labette's ship pulled away now. I adjusted the angle of the cannon and lit the fuse. The cannon roared and kindling flew from Labette's ship.

My fortune knew no limits as the gun next to me was already packed and loaded. The crackle of the fuse was followed by another roar. I was not given time to fire the third cannon. Distant booms sent me against the hull of the ship and into the warm rising sea. Exhausted, I fell to her willingly.

Morning

Chapter Ten

As storm clouds gather around the flagship and her captured brigantine, Admiral Charles Price records the life of Captain Hook in vivid detail, as it is recounted. The story of Hook sinking into the sea went beyond the admiral's patience and pierced his composure.

"Rubbish," Admiral Price mutters into his tea. Captain Hook stops mid-breath and turns sharply to meet the admiral's eyes.

"I've learned to be more careful with that word, Admiral," Hook cautions, "and the arrogance that goes along with it."

The silent moments that pass between them are broken by the entrance of the older crewman carrying two lit candles. In the fading light of the storm, the cell aboard the *Triumph* is nearly as black as pitch without their gentle flicker.

"This is hogwash," the admiral stammers on. "If what you say is true, you'd be dead at sea before even becoming a man."

"Death is only one of many obstacles I have overcome,"

Hooks sneers.

"If you are not going to take this seriously," Admiral Price cautions, "then I should remind you that these foolish words are recorded as your last."

"What's wrong, Admiral?" Hook mocks. "Have I not sufficiently entertained you in our time together?" He breaks his gaze for a moment to check the time.

"That watch," Admiral Price nods. "How did you get it?" Captain Hook looks up and smiles.

"I'm getting there, Admiral," Hook says. "Are you in a rush?"

"Give it to me," Admiral Price says. He holds his hand out just beyond the bars of the cell.

"Excuse me?" Hook asks after several stunned seconds.

"You check it too often for my taste." He motions for the older crewman to unlock the door. "Get it for me," the admiral commands. The crewman fumbles with the keys before sliding the gate across with a clang. The crewman starts toward Captain Hook but pauses again and looks back at the admiral and the larger crewman.

"What are you waiting for?" the admiral scolds.

"Yes. What indeed?" Captain Hook snaps at the older crewman. "Come and get what the admiral has asked for." The older crewman storms into the cell and rams the butt of his sword into Hook's ribs, doubling him over. The larger crewman lifts Hook up and holds him against the bars while the older one retrieves the watch from his pocket. When finished with the assault, the crewman drops Captain Hook to the floor in a heap.

"Was that all necessary?" Hook says through a bloodied smile.

"You've had it coming," the larger crewman responds with a smirk.

"Waiting to do that for some time now, have we?"

"Aye. Longer than you know, Captain," the crewman says with a broad grin.

"Enough," the admiral interrupts. "If this really is the watch of Jonathan Hoodkins, then you have no rights to it."

"I have no rights to my father's watch?" Hook asks.

"I challenge your claim to be his son as heartily as I challenge your ravings of meeting this Peter Pan, whatever he is."

"Have you ever seen a shade, Admiral?" Hook asks. "One that passes just outside of sight, but when you look for it, it isn't there? If so, then you, too, have seen Peter Pan."

"Madness," Admiral Price scoffs.

"Not one for fantasy, are you? Well, if you find it hard to believe what I have said so far," Captain Hook leads, "wait until you hear of how I returned from death."

The Tale of the Island

Chapter Eleven

My body was thrown into the current of time and space. In it I rode waves of ethereal matter. I kept my eyes closed to truly feel each movement. The waves took me higher and I floated as if pulled by an unknown source. Finally, I opened my eyes and saw an endless field of stars and streaks of colors so beautiful I began to tear. Then I noticed, flying next to me, was a familiar imp in tattered green clothes.

"What is going on here, Peter?" I asked. My frustration overran my sense of wonder. "Where am I and what are you doing?" The assault of questions staggered him. He paused for a small eternity before answering.

"I do this sometimes," he said at last, "you know, travel with you. Most of the way, anyway."

The answer was more confusing than the floating and limitless vision of stars and moons. I searched for a question to help me understand his meaning, but came up with only the most basic response, "Most of the way where?"

"Heaven," he replied. "You died."

The words hit me like cannon fire. Cannon Fire! Then I remembered. My mind flooded with memories of my final day. I recalled the pirates, the damage, my father taken from me by that betraying Heath Ashley. I had been so drawn in by the feeling of death that I'd forgotten the cause.

"I don't get to do this for everyone," Pan continued, "but I never miss it when one of my friends dies."

This statement brought my thoughts to a halt. Once again, I found myself searching for a response. "How many of your friends died?"

Pan thought for a moment. "All of them."

"All of them?" I gasped. "So you have no more friends."

"No, I have plenty," he smiled. "More are born every day."

"So you just keep doing this? Wait for new friends to crop up, have your fun, then escort them to hell?"

"Heaven," Pan corrected as a shooting star sailed over our heads. "Most children are scared."

"I'm not most children," I lied. I was terrified, but it would be poor form to show it. I stared into the endless gaping darkness between the bright points of light and knew that this trip was not right for me. Not yet, anyway. My mother, William, and Emily needed me.

"Take me back," I told him. I took mild amusement in watching his face go pale at the suggestion.

"We can't just go back," Pan stammered. He looked more confused than ever. I pressed the advantage.

"Like hell you can't. You fly, disappear, and cross the barrier between heaven and earth. You can surely take me home." He looked completely dumbfounded now. I feared that I might have reached the limit of his intelligence. My only hope was that he didn't completely shut down or worse, run off and leave me to float here for a thousand lifetimes.

"But that's not where your body is," he finally said.

He was right about that. In fact, I had no idea where my body was aside from a coordinate on a map.

"Then put me back in my body," I told him, "I'll get myself home." His face twisted with indecision. I decided to push him in the direction I wanted him to go. "What's the matter? Haven't you ever taken someone back from heaven before?"

"Well, no," Pan said, "I haven't."

"Oh, okay. If you don't think you can do it…"

"I can do anything!" Pan shouted. "But if you go back, you'll grow up," he said with a newfound sadness. "We wouldn't be able to play anymore."

"That's not a priority for me right now, Peter," I snapped. "I have important things to do."

Pan scowled. "You're already sounding like a grown up."

"I guess dying does that to you," I told him. And with that, we were on our way through the barrier between death and life.

Chapter Twelve

The pillow was coarse and I reached for covers that weren't there. Waves crashed against my feet, telling me to move. My head throbbed as though it were on fire. My hand felt around my shoulder and touched something rough, wet, and warm. The wound was already scabbed over and caked with sand.

The cuts on my arms scraped against the sand as I rose to my feet. I placed one foot in front of the other and began to explore my new home. The beach was golden and still. Beyond it, a row of trees guarded a thick forest.

Only the waves made noise as they gently lapped the shoreline. I stumbled to it to wash my cuts. The salt stung me and I saw what treasures the beach truly held. A bloated uniformed body drifted on the water. Its green skin and gaped expression mirrored my own shock.

Bodies of soldiers and pirates floated by me. Some crashed onto the sand while others were gently placed. The sea randomly decided which body got which treatment and there was no discrimination between the two. It didn't matter whether you lived a life of service to your country or to your own purse; the sea decided your fate and all men ended up face down in the sand eventually.

William. My wounds made me forget all about him and my promise to Emily. The thought snapped me into action and I began turning bodies. It didn't occur to me to only turn the smaller ones. In my frantic haste, I flipped everything that washed ashore: a crewman, a pirate, another pirate, Mr. Stevenson.

When I turned the body of my father, I expected the world to collapse around me but, strangely, it didn't. I took a moment to examine him. He was missing an arm and most of his rib cage, but the rest of his body held together. I stared at him for untold minutes before I realized that I hadn't shed a single tear. I knew I should feel something. Grief? No. Pain? No. Loss? Nothing. I dragged him further up shore to tend to him later.

After an hour of searching, I found William up the shoreline. I stalked to his motionless body. He was laying on a piece of timber. This was a good sign, but I didn't let it get to me. I had believed several of the men were lying on wood only to find that they had been impaled on the broken boards. As I got closer, I noticed a slight rising and falling in his chest. He was wet and the side of his body was purple and broken, but he was warm to the touch.

I allowed myself a quick sigh of relief. I pulled William onto the dune to prevent him from being washed away and turned my attention to the next step: survival. Luck was with me, as three barrels of grain and preserved meats washed up on the shore soon after. By the time William woke, I had already gathered wood for a fire.

"What happened?" he asked after stirring for hours. He saw me attempting to start our fire and couldn't resist a comment. "You never did that right, James." He began to shift his weight to his side.

"Don't move," I told him. He tried to stand anyway and howled in pain. With each cough, blood spilled from his mouth. Stubborn as anyone I ever knew, he managed to work his way over to me.

"Give me those," he said. Even injured, William could start and spread a fire faster than a child's laughter. After seconds of agony, the fire was lit and he gathered his strength to ask me again, "What happened?"

"The ship broke up against rocks in the water," I lied. He would be better off forgetting the battle all together. I'd be grateful for the chance to forget.

"That's not what happened," he said. His memories returned to him quickly, and with them the sights and sounds of battle. Tears welled up and soaked his already clammy and bruised cheeks. I left him to cry so that I might bury my father in peace.

The search for a proper burial site within the forest began with a deep breath. I dragged Father's body away from the beach and onto more solid ground. I didn't know how long we were going to call this island home and the last thing I wanted was to have a storm unearth his grave. The ground behind the thin line of trees was wet and dark. The brush that scratched at my legs was so thick that my feet disappeared as they stepped down into it.

A tall palm tree caught my eye. The markings on it were those of a Spaniard. I memorized the words, but not the meaning: *Agua de Eterna Juventud*. A pool of fresh water bubbled just fifty paces from the tree line. The cliff was framed with hanging vines, and at the end of a wide path leading to it was a dark cave. From the mouth of the cave, all along the path, a stream of water trickled down to the spring. It was a truly beautiful sight, but that didn't interest me at the moment. Water is life and I thirsted for it. I knelt at the banks and drank deep mouthfuls. I brought William over to the spring and made sure he drank as well.

Happy to have found shelter and fresh water, I decided to take my father another thirty paces east of the spring. The only things of value that my father still had on him were his watch and a gold coin on a silver chain. I could not read the markings on the coin, but it was clearly not a doubloon. Neither of these would be helpful on the island but I decided to take them anyway. That watch had been in my family for generations and I was certain that my father would have wanted me to have it. I placed it in my pocket, hanged the coin around my neck, and began digging.

I had never been to a funeral before. My prayer was crude, but honest. I thanked Father for his service to me in this life and wished him well in the next. I asked that he watch over me from afar so that he may pay closer attention to my mother.

I tried again to feel some form of pain over my father's death. I began forcing my mind to feel grief or sadness, but the harder I tried the more my mind returned to a single emotion: anger. My mind was consumed with a single thought. Jesse Labette was the pirate who murdered my father and Heath Ashley was the captain who abandoned him to his death. I dropped to my knees and let the anger well up inside of me and fill the empty spaces. The kernel was small, for now, but I was pleased with myself for finding a hook to hang onto.

Chapter Thirteen

The bodies began disappearing the next morning. At first, I thought it was the tide, but no tide I knew had ever left a trail of blood. The mystery deepened three weeks in as I came upon William boiling water in an old pot that washed ashore. As the steam kissed his dirty face, I heard him singing like a schoolboy again. The song started in low tones and built as I approached.

"We're all alone on island shores,
With nothing left but rot.
But something good is boiling now,
Inside my rusty pot."

"Look, James, we're civilized again," he said. I looked over into the pot and saw three eggs but not any type I had ever seen before. These were somehow different. Spotted. Larger.

"So it seems," I said. Boiling eggs was a far cry from civilization, but we needed to keep our spirits up. This wasn't a difficult task since our stay on the island had gone very well so far. We had barrels of preserved food and as much fresh water as we could drink. My injuries healed within a day and William was on his feet the next morning. I was glad that I was wrong about how hurt he really was.

"It's better than searching for rats or dead fish," he said, tossing me one of the eggs.

"And how is that you have come across these treasures?" I asked. I cracked the coarse shell and dug out the meat. "I haven't seen many animals on this island."

"Up in the cave," William responded.

"Show me."

He took me behind the spring, where the dirt and leaves clung tightly to the rock wall like Peter's and Tinkerbell's clothing, and pointed to the stream of water that trickled from the mouth of the cave.

I had been so preoccupied with food and shelter that I had not even thought to go exploring. As William ran into the mouth of the cave, I saw that he was not as burdened as I was. He took advantage of every opportunity without thought and without planning. I envied that sometimes.

William led me about twenty paces into the cave. It was deeper than I thought. On the outside it seemed that after about twenty or twenty-five paces I should have reached the back wall. I found this curious, but quickly dismissed the idea as I saw the water trickle down into the pool below. Water had to go downhill so we must have been going up an incline. We got only a few more paces in when the darkness made it difficult to see.

"Why don't you grab some fire from the camp before we go further?"

"There's no need," William said. "The nest is only a few feet more." In an offshoot of the cave, away from the stream of water, we came across a dirt patch dug into the cave floor. It was an empty, sad hole now, but it clearly was the nest that William found earlier. I moved to inspect it more closely, but William blocked me with an arm across the chest.

I watched as a bead of sweat ripened on his forehead and traveled the length of his cheek. My eyes followed as it rolled to his chin, dangled, then dropped to the dirt below.

There, sprawled out on the cave floor, was what looked like a suit of armor, only dark and seemingly made of rough leather. I knew it by the drawings in my books and the stories of my mother and father. This crocodile was easily twice my height and length and broader than the two of us were shoulder to shoulder. He was either sleeping or lying in wait. It was impossible to know which when you looked into its cold, black eyes.

To its right, a pile of bones and tattered uniforms screamed their silent warning. In fluid, silent motion, we eased out of the cave. Once outside, we sprinted for the beach. In my terror, I managed to keep up with William until there was sand between my toes. Then, my body collapsed in a heap.

"I don't ever want to see that thing again," William panted. He leaned over and helped me stand. "Do you think it has our scent?"

"Are you willing to wait and find out?" I asked between gasps. Knowing looks passed between us. His face went white with shock.

"You're out of your mind!" William shouted. "There's no way we can kill that thing."

"Why not?" I asked. "We know the beast. We know where it lies and we know what it eats."

"Yeah, us," he said as he stormed down to the shoreline.

"Only if we let it," I told him. "If we control its movements, we control its fate."

"You saw the size of that thing!" William said. He turned and begged me with his eyes, trying to convince me that the job was too difficult.

"Yeah, which means the trap only has to be twelve-by-seven," I said, proving him wrong. I walked down to him by the water and put my hand on his shoulder. "It just ate, so that gives us some time."

"Time for what?" he asked.

"Time to dig."

Chapter Fourteen

We worked through the night and by sunrise, everything was in place. Fresh sunlight hit our backs as we stood at the cave's mouth. I was reminded of one of the stories in my literature books about St. George's adventure in Libya. There, he slew a dragon of terrible might. William and I were about to do the same, which made sense in some twisted way.

In this fantastic world of Peter Pan, why wouldn't I have to fight my own dragon? I was almost disappointed that it was not flying, with black leathery wings, or breathing fire that lit the night up like day. All I needed to do was coax him to come and get me.

"How do we even know that he's still in here?" William asked.

"Look down," I told him. "There are no fresh tracks." Our harried footsteps from our sprint last night were the last impressions in the dirt leading out of the cave. "Get ready."

We moved to our positions on either side of the cave

mouth. I tucked my father's coin into my shoe so as not to lose it. The watch sat heavily in my pants pocket.

We sacrificed more than just a night's sleep. Two day's worth of rations sat atop eight-foot sticks. My blood pounded loudly as I thought again of what we were planning to do here. I was only distracted from the pounding in my ears when William broke our patient silence.

"James," he said. "Why did you lie to me?"

"What are you talking about?" I snapped at him. "There are no fresh croc tracks and we don't have time for me to explain the plan to you again." He backed away a little as if hit with an invisible force. I couldn't do this alone and I needed him focused or we'd both end up eaten. "What don't you understand?"

"When I first woke up, you told me that the ship wrecked against rocks," he said, now meeting my eyes. "Why would you lie to me?" It was now my turn to be hit with an invisible force. The guilt of lying to him paled compared to the shame of not having a good reason for it. My stomach twisted and I gave him the best answer I had.

"Sometimes, William, the fantasy is easier to live with than the truth." He nodded, even though I wasn't sure he knew what I meant. I motioned towards the cave, signaling the start of the plan.

We began by casting the line. William pulled three stones from his pocket and threw them into the cave one by one. The first two clanged against the rocky wall, but the third one thudded. Something rustled briefly in the darkness and then became purposely silent. Moments later, bones rattled against one another and the beast emerged from the darkness.

It was as I saw him in the previous night. He was armored with thick scales and bared the deadliest row of teeth in his crushing jaws. He hissed at us as he advanced.

The plan continued as we stood at either side of the croc. We passed his attention back and forth between our bait. When he got too close to me, I raised the bait too high for him to reach and William lowered his bait to attract its attention. We led it down a grooved path so that we were always on elevated terrain. It was a simple trap for a dumb animal. The going was slower than I expected, but the pace was not important.

The plan was flawless, if not for the human factor. William became impatient and let the croc get too close. It lunged and caught William's bait in its mouth. The wood splintered in the beast's jaws and we lost one day's worth of food. William scrambled up the nearest tree with a curse and half of a stick.

William was a fast climber, but the croc was a skilled hunter. He looked up at William and braced his front claws against the trunk of the tree. He jumped and snapped his jaws loudly just below William's foot. William was safe for now, but the croc was a patient killer and had all the time in the world to wait for William to climb, jump, or fall out of the tree from lack of sleep or food.

"Idiot," I muttered under my breath. The croc immediately turned to face me, as if the comment was made at his expense. Remembering that I still had my bait, I decided to try killing this monster on my own.

With two men, this plan was doable. With a third, it'd be a cinch. Alone, I was one small mistake away from death. I had to quicken my pace to account for my partner's absence. I raised and lower the baited stick, careful not to leave myself open for attack. Distance and pace were now everything and my endurance held it all together.

Thick blood slogged through my veins as I backed myself

towards the trap. It was dug in a spot on the island where a thick line of trees blocked access to either side of the path. Using the last of my strength, I climbed against the tree line and leapt over the trap to the other side. Once there, I crumbled to my knees as my physical body gave in to exhaustion. I placed the bait on the ground in front of me and stared the beast in his black eyes.

As it glared at me, a thousand possibilities ran through my mind. What if the sticks were too weak or too strong? What if the croc wasn't heavy enough? What if the ditch wasn't deep enough? What if he climbed out? The answer to all of these was simple. I die.

I was not the man that St. George was. I had no sword or shield or suit of armor. I only had a knife, a single pistol with only one shot, and a crude tiger trap. Fortunately, the croc was no fire-breathing dragon of legend. He was an animal, nothing more.

The croc moved slowly over the trap at first, readying his jaws to snap shut on me. Then, just as he braced himself to leap, the branches gave way under his weight. The sharp sticks underneath impaled it at four points. The crackle of leaves and twigs muffled its death cry. It writhed for minutes before it finally died. I breathed deeply and promised myself that the next time I had to lead a monster to its death, I would plan more carefully.

Chapter Fifteen

The croc proved to be a hearty meal, giving us three days of full stomachs. We ate the whole thing, not wasting a single part. We couldn't afford to since the next meal was not promised and we had to keep our strength up. The days ahead would be our most trying.

The cave that William and I made into our home was in a steep rock wall that overlooked the spring. That cliff was the tallest point of the island. Standing on top of it, I saw the coming storm.

The first gusts of autumn carried with it the knowledge that I missed registration at Eton. When registration is up again next fall, I'll be fourteen, too old to claim the scholarship I earned this cycle.

Birds called out to one another before darting off into the sky. William watched them as they flew away. I knew enough to look in the other direction. Dark clouds gathered miles to the south.

The wind whistled a silent warning. Waves picked up pace. Soon, the gentle temper of the island became menacing. We had hours at most, so I set us to work immediately.

William and I had a good give and take. I requested. He fetched. I assembled. Over the past few weeks, we made chairs, a table, and a workbench. Now, we made traps.

The traps we made weren't for the animals that live on this island. Those we made weeks ago. Instead, I hoped to collect what fish the storm would surely bring in. I weaved vines into a net and tethered it to the trees at the island's southern inlet.

The clouds came in like a thick grey sheet within hours, tucking the sun away long before its bedtime. And like a child, the sun peeked through the cracks to get a last look in on what it was missing.

It's that thought of childhood that brought my mind to William. He had fully recovered from near death. His color returned before that first night. His broken bones and open gashes all mended in days. The first clash of thunder snapped my mind back to the present.

We began to bring the barrels inside to wait out the storm. I dragged the last of the barrels through the mouth of the cave and bumped into William, who stood dumbfounded.

"What are you staring at?" I scolded. But when I turned, I finally saw the state of our home. Our barrels were toppled and shattered. The cots we made from tattered clothing, leaves, and branches were torn to ribbons. Our stores of food were gone. We had nothing.

"What madness is this?" I asked.

William shrugged, "Maybe some animals got in here..."

"And tore up our beds? No, this was deliberate," I told him.

"Someone wanted to do this to us."

"Someone?" William asked. "You mean there is someone else here?"

"I'm not sure if he really is a 'someone', but I'm almost certain that he's here," I told him.

"James, what are you talking about?" William's face twisted in the same way that Emily's did that morning I told her about Peter Pan. I resolved to hold myself to the promise I made not to talk about Pan until I had absolute proof. It wasn't in William's limited philosophy to allow him to understand. Not yet, anyway.

"Nothing," I lied. "I'm just spooked is all." He nodded and turned back to look further into the cave. "Stay here and get a fire going. I'll check if we forgot anything."

As I made my way to my father's grave, terrible thoughts came to mind. William and I made life on the island possible, but for how long? There was no means of escape. No source of food was certain or sustainable. Now, if Peter Pan was having fun at our expense, how else could this end except with our deaths?

"Father," I started. "I don't think we're going to make it off of this island." I laughed joylessly to myself as I realized how much easier it was to talk to my father now that he was dead. Out of habit, I reached into my pocket and flicked the gold watch open. The loud ticking pierced through the gathering storm, focusing me. "I'm being strong for William, but even he has to realize that we'll never see home again." Tears of rage ran down my cheeks as I snapped the watch shut. "I'm sorry that I'll never avenge you. The monsters that deserved to die go on living while I waste away here." There was shame in my doubt. Somehow I felt that I had to speak those words aloud to hear how unlike me defeat really was.

A new resolve burned within my chest and I allowed myself to build the fantasy that kept me strong. I thought of my mother, sitting by the fire clutching her old scarf. She rocked slowly back and forth with each sob. I watched her face light up with joy as William and I burst through the door. She held me close and called to Emily, who came in from the dining hall and ran into my arms. It was all perfect. The way it was meant to be.

A sudden rustling to my right startled me. Nimble feet pattered on the soft dirt. The pace was quick and playful. My first guess was logical but entirely wrong.

"William?" I called. "What in blazes are you doing?" My error must have been irresistibly funny, because it was followed by a familiar and infuriating giggle. It was unmistakable.

"Peter!" I cried. "Pan! Show yourself!" I challenged. The rustling stopped. Hidden behind the brush, two eyes lit up in the gathering darkness. They were not as I remembered them from the night we met.

A beast lunged for me just as I began backing away. Its jaws snapped inches from my face. I tumbled to the ground, but recovered my footing quickly and drew my knife. My heart raced as I finally saw the full measure of the creature.

This crocodile covered the distance of the brush in two steps. Its length and breadth were easily twice that of the one William and I killed. Something ancient and angry stared back at me from behind her black, dead eyes. We could never dig a ditch big enough.

We stared at each other for minutes. Her jaws opened and closed slightly as if she would speak at any moment. Part of me wished that she would. Talking crocodiles would fit quite nicely in this twisted world of fantasy and horror. I moved to the right and she moved to match. I moved to the left, she moved and advanced. There was nothing to do but stand still and wait for her to come get me.

With a howl, William swung in from my right, wielding a tall pointed branch. He did his best to get in front of me and draw the crocodile's attention but it didn't work.

"What's got it so mad?" he asked.

"She's really got it out for me, doesn't she?" I said. Of the three ways I could get out of this alive, only one involved not sacrificing William to the crocodile. It did, however, involve the sacrifice of my only pistol shot. I drew my pistol from my belt and aimed it at the croc's head.

"How do you know this one is the female?" William asked.

"We ate her eggs and killed her mate," I smirked. "Only a mother would be so angry." There was no time to plan and no room to maneuver. It was unlikely that this shot would kill the animal. At most, it would scare her away or startle her enough for us to make good our escape.

As I drew the hammer back, the beast paused. She looked to the sky and breathed in deeply. She hissed at us again and disappeared into the thick underbrush. William and I looked to the darkened clouds and felt the first drops of rain.

"What happened?" William asked.

"She's hiding from the storm," I told him. "The croc could have killed us just now, but there'd be no joy in it for her. The coming storm would have hastened the taste of her revenge." She didn't need to speak for me to understand her perfectly. "Get into the cave. We're not safe here."

Chapter Sixteen

Wind and water pounded the rock outside as William and I sat for hours and watched the fire make shadows dance against the rocky wall. We didn't talk. We didn't move. We just watched.

The quiet gave me time to think again of how oddly fortunate our lives were on the island. If it were not for the fresh water spring and the barrels of food that washed ashore, we would never have survived this long. Now, the cave provided the ideal shelter from the storm.

My trance was broken when the fire began to die into smoldering embers.

"We need to keep it burning," I told him. William snapped out of a waking sleep and gathered kindling.

"Why?" he asked. "It isn't cold here, just wet." I grabbed the dry twigs and snapped them before setting them onto the pile.

"The fire isn't for us," I said. The sticks caught and light filled the cave more brightly than before. I pointed into the darkness outside, "It's for her."

"The croc? Where?" William stared for several seconds more. "I don't see anything except for a fallen tree trunk at the cave opening." At that moment, the tree trunk blinked and snorted. Her eyes flashed a cold reflection of the flames.

"My god," William gasped. "How long has she been there?"

"About two hours," I told him as I added another dry log to the pile.

"What are we going to do?" he asked me without taking his eyes off of the beast. He stared for another few moments before speaking again. "I mean, you can't be thinking that we can kill her."

"Right now, we wait her out," I told him. "She's looking for shelter. The fire is the only thing that is keeping her away and that's your job." He turned to me and looked down.

"Good, because you're doing it all wrong again," he said as the color returned to his face. He knelt by the fire and made two quick adjustments. "You need to let air in or you'll smother the flame." In seconds, the blaze was hot and bright.

"At least we know the fire is in good hands," I said with a smirk. He smiled as he hopped over the thin stream of water to look for more wood to burn.

"I don't blame her for wanting this cave back," William said with a grin. "It's warm. It's dry. There is even a way to drain rain water out from the storm." I didn't think much of the comment at first, but the longer I let it sit in my mind, the more a question burned to the surface.

"If that is true," I thought aloud, "then why is there always a stream even when it isn't raining?" The question puzzled William and sparked even greater curiosity in me. The fresh water that made up the spring outside came from within the cave. There wasn't any more water flowing now than usual. Was this water really from the storm or from another source entirely? I realized that, in the time since we killed the male croc, I never thought to venture further into the cave.

"I'm exploring," I told William. "Stay here and keep the fire lit. We don't want her back in here." I made a small torch and followed the water upstream.

Although the island itself was scarcely a mile in length, I must have covered half of that distance in the brief moments of my exploration. By all rational sense, I should have been outside behind the cliff when I first stopped to relight the torch. The cave had been black as pitch since I first left William to guard the entrance. As the fire died in my hands, a faint glow at the far end of the cave got steadily brighter.

The madness of this island was dizzying. There was no way that there could be a second entrance to the cave. There was no such opening outside.

As I approached, I found a small pond, no more than twenty paces in diameter. The rock wall shot straight down, closing it off at the back. The water trickled past my feet toward the mouth of the cave. The water had to be coming from a natural wellspring underneath.

With the mystery solved, I turned to make my way back to tell William. But as my fingers traced the wall, I caught a carving in the rock. Like the tree outside, the words were those of a Spaniard: País de Nunca Lamás. I didn't know what it meant, but I studied enough Latin to know that País was a form of the word land. Nunca looked like some form of no or not.

My mind rolled the words over again and again. *Land No?* That made no sense. *Not Land? No Land?* It seemed likely that someone stranded here would curse his fate. My eyes widened as I looked at the carving again. Shock tore down another barrier between what was and what couldn't be.

Never Land.

"But that's impossible," I whispered.

My fingers traced the cracked edges of the rock wall repeatedly. There were no seams. No hinges. No openings.

The light from the wellspring rippled against the walls, drawing my attention back to it. William could hold his breath far longer than me. My first thought was to run back and get him, but I couldn't lie to him again nor could I tell him about Peter. If I couldn't prove Pan's existence, I would not make myself into a fool yet again. I took off my shoes and over shirt and waded into the water.

I swam to the bottom and found that I didn't have far to go. Several feet down, I came to a passage much wider than I expected. Four men could swim side by side through the opening.

Nearly a minute later, just as I reached the edge of how long I could hold my breath, I surfaced. I coughed, wiped my eyes, and looked around. I was in another cave with more dark rocky walls, but this time the water led in from an outside source. I rose from the pond and followed it.

The crashing sound up ahead told me that there was a waterfall long before I saw it. This was clearly the source of the water on the island, but where was it coming from? Spray from the rocks stung my face and arms as I worked my way around.

Once free, I turned and saw Neverland for the first time.

My breath fled into the noonday air as tears streamed down my face. When I did breathe back in, my lungs were filled with a honey-scented sweetness. Worry, anger, and pain melted from me and I became too heavy to stand.

What stunned me was not the fantastic, but the distinguishable clarity of the common. Everything looked as fresh and vivid as a new uniform. The grass was the most vivid green. The flowers were a vibrant blue and violet. The water, however, had no color. It was completely clear regardless of depth.

I rose from my knees and took my first steps in this new world. I walked without knowing that I took a single step but caught myself in time to get my bearings and see beyond the waterfall. Grassy hills and forests covered the land. On all sides the endless expanse of water mocked me. Even here, I was stranded without hope.

I turned to head back when a rustling startled me. Fearing the croc, I ducked behind a four foot mushroom and peered around the corner to identify my stalker.

The forest ceased to move as if begging me to come out of hiding. The thick blood of my veins pounded in my ears with each passing moment. Suddenly, a voice assaulted me from above.

"I found you, Slightly! You're it!" squealed the upside down boy.

"Who?" I shot back. His eyes opened wide with shock and he spilled off of the mushroom cap onto the grass.

"You're not Slightly," the boy said.

"I know that," I told him. "Who are you?"

"They call me Nibs. I'm one of the Lost Boys."

Chapter Seventeen

"Nibs?" I asked. "What kind of name is that?" The boy got up off of the ground and dusted himself off. I didn't see the point, seeing how he was covered in filth from head to toe.

"It's my name and I'm proud of it," he said with a smile. "What's yours?"

"James," I told him. He's younger than me and smaller too. The knife tucked away in his belt told me more about his life here than anything else.

"You're not from here," he said. I couldn't help but laugh out loud. "Well, if you're not from Neverland, how did you get here?" I pointed to the waterfall and his face went white. "The croc's cave? No one goes in there. She's a monster."

"I know. I've seen her." I took a step back toward the waterfall and a twig snapped behind the bushes, followed by hushed whispers. "You said there were others?"

He nodded to the tree line and underbrush. One by one, dirty children emerged out into the open and surrounded me.

"We're the Lost Boys," Nibs said. I looked from one to the other until my eyes settled on a familiar face.

"Donald?" I asked. "Donald Sotheby?" There was no mistaking his curly hair and dim expression. "My God, I can't believe I have found you." But as I moved to greet him, the others raised their weapons of war against me.

"What is the meaning of this?" I said as they looked me over carefully.

"Found me?" Donald asked. "I've been here as long as I remember. And my name's Curly."

"Nibs," the one with the panda hat and blackened eye said, "where did you find this one?"

"He says he came from the cave behind the waterfall, Tootles," Nibs responded. "He says he'd seen the croc." The boys gasped all at once. I decided to ignore their foolishness and turn my attention back to my old schoolmate.

"Donald, you were in my class at Port Royal. You disappeared over a year ago." He looked to Nibs and then back to me.

"I don't know what you are talking about," he said, shaking his head. The boys looked to one another and kept their sharpened sticks and knives pointed at me.

"Your father is a doctor in town. Mine is … was a captain." I searched for some recognition in his eyes, but found only pools of emptiness. "We looked for you."

A stifled "thank you" and a shrug was the best he offered in response. Maybe he had some sort of accident or a bump on the head has affected his memory. I decided to use another boy as an example.

"Nibs, where are you from?" I asked. His face twisted as though it were an odd question.

"What do you mean? I'm from Neverland," he said.

"I mean before Neverland. You had to have come from somewhere." I saw that I was going to have to guide him to the answer I was looking for. "You know how I came through the cave? If you didn't come through the cave, then how did you get here? How did you get to Neverland?" His eyes lit up and he puffed his chest with confidence.

"I was brought here," he said confidently. He then made a broad wave towards all of the boys and said, "We all were."

"Brought here?" I asked. "Who would bring you here?" The answer came to me before any of the boys could speak. Memories of endless fields of stars and moons flashed before my eyes as I said the name of the only boy I knew who was capable of bringing a child across creation, "Pan."

A wind from the shore cut through the trees and shook tired limbs. Countless jostled birds took flight, blotting out the sun. Among their cries, I heard a rooster crow followed by the patter of two nimble feet landing fast between the boys and me. They all gasped again, lowered their weapons, and stared in amazement.

"Wow, you've found me," Peter Pan called out. "I am so happy. Now we can play all we want, forever."

"Forever?" I asked him, still stunned by his sudden appearance. With the birds gone, the sun lit up his hair and features.

"Of course, forever," he told me, "and besides, I'm tired of just playing with Tiger Lily and her Indians."

"So this truly is Neverland?" I asked him. Pan looked at his boys before they all doubled over in laughter.

"But of course it is," Peter said, still rolling on the grass. "Where else would I be, silly?"

The question was a bit naive after everything I'd seen. It just seemed that since the first night we met, Pan had shown me the impossible. If I'd only been able to fly that first night, perhaps I'd have seen many more wonders.

At that moment, my eyes caught Donald's gaze. Again, I searched his face but there seemed to be nothing left of my friend behind those eyes. My mind raced to the only possible conclusion.

"I don't know, perhaps taking children from their homes?" I sneered. The question took Peter by complete surprise. His face grew stern as he rose to his feet. I pointed to Donald.

"His name is Donald Sotheby and he was my schoolmate," I told him.

"Curly?" Peter asked, annoyed.

"He disappeared the night we first met," I continued. "You took him because I couldn't fly, didn't you?"

"His name is Curly and he wants to be here," Peter said, now hovering inches off of the ground.

"He wants this, does he?" I asked. "Mindless? Dirty? No memories? Is this what you would have me be, Peter? These boys have families. They have mothers and fathers."

"What's a family when you have Neverland?" he said, soaring over our heads. The boys, Donald included, watched in wonder. "Battles and adventure! Treasure and games! It's an eternal childhood."

"It's an eternal servitude," I called out to him. Peter did another loop in the air to the boys' delight. I turned to Donald and grabbed his wrist. "Come, I'll get you home."

Seeing this, Peter stopped his show and swooped down between us. He landed on the mushroom cap, drew his short sword, and raised it to the sky.

"Lost Boys! Fall in!" he commanded. Like an obedient dog, Curly left my side and took his place in the formation. They stood at attention and awaited their next order.

"You're all fools!" I shouted at them. "Without your memories, you are truly lost." I turned back to the waterfall and Peter flew around to block the way.

"Why don't you stay with us?" His voice was soft and kind again. "Aren't you lost, too?" Something ancient and unnatural stared back at me from behind his eyes. I didn't know what he truly was, but Peter Pan was no mere boy.

"I am not lost, Peter. I'm stranded. There's a difference," I told him. I moved again to the cave and he again moved in my way. The temperature dropped suddenly. Clouds rolled in and the sky became dark.

"Why are you doing this?" I asked him. "With a thought, you could send William and me back to our homes. I have to get back and if you are not going to help me then I will have to do it myself." With inhuman speed, he placed a hand on my shoulder and leaned in close.

"You won't survive as you are," he said. "If it isn't the croc, it'll be something else." Whether this was a threat, a warning, or a trick, I knew he was right. Our stores of food were running low and William and I risked starving within weeks. One look back to the Lost Boys gave me all the answers I needed.

"I'd rather die as I am now than live for centuries like them." With a deep breath, I pushed past him and into the cave, leaving Neverland behind.

Chapter Eighteen

The storm passed, causing little damage. Its wake, however, devastated us.

When the skies finally cleared, we emerged from the cave to downed trees and upturned beaches. Paths we had walked for months no longer existed and in their place, new paths were carved. I used these new paths to check on my father's grave site.

William set up the fire in the mouth of the cave to keep burning while we were out. As large as it was, this croc was not as bold as to attack while we were together. Still, we made our way with caution.

The tree with the carved words was split in half down the middle. Nothing of the old Spaniard's words remained. Thirty paces east, my fears were abated as we found my father's grave undisturbed. The breath I released carried with it more worry than I would have thought. My shoulders slumped and I allowed myself a second breath of respite.

"James!" William called out from behind the brush. My

heart leapt again into my throat and my pulse pounded with the fear of what might be. Pistol drawn, I pounced on William's position.

I approached William who was hurriedly digging a mound in the dirt. He called out to me again and began to bang at something hard. Wood splintered and creaked as he tore the lid off of an old chest, revealing gold as bright as the sun and speckled with gems like the night's sky.

"James!" he cried. "We're rich!" His face broadened with a grin brighter than all the treasure in the royal court. Bile churned in my stomach and I lost the battle to compose my temper.

"We are wealthy men," I bit. "With that kind of money, maybe we can charter a ship home?" His eyes dimmed as his folly was laid bare. He got up and kicked the chest over in a rage against his own foolishness.

Three weeks passed and every day was a struggle. William and I carried on by dodging the croc and fishing when we could. Both of us were needed to stay alive and we became quite good at knowing what the other was thinking.

One morning, it ended in shouts and gunpowder.

William shook me from sleep. His eyes were wide with panic and he was out of breath from running.

"The far side… of the island…" was all he stammered at first. His next breath made real the fear we'd been desperate to avoid. "Pirates."

We leapt from the cave and climbed up the vines onto the overhang above the mouth of our new home. From there, we could see the far shore. Off in the distance was a colossal three-masted frigate with a black flag above the crow's nest. I didn't need to look at the design of the flag to know that William was right.

"How far off are they?" William asked. I reached into my

pocket and flicked my father's watch open.

"They'll land in fifteen minutes," I told him. "If they head straight to us, it'll take them another ten." I snapped it shut and stuffed it into my pocket.

"Why come at us?" he asked.

"We have their treasure," I told him. A smug look overtook his face. "The gold has value to those who can use it."

"But the treasure wasn't buried here," he said. "Won't they go there first?"

"True, but once they see proof of our being here, they will come after us." I looked him over to make sure he understood. His face went red with frustration, then white with panic.

"The cave is the only place to hide on the island," he said. "They'll know we're here. There is nowhere else to go." I almost corrected him. There was another place to go, but he wasn't ready to go there yet and I was not ready to go back. My thoughts drifted away to my encounter with the Lost Boys for a moment until a more mischievous thought entered my mind. My face broadened into a smile as a plan formed.

"Who knew?" I smirked at William. "That gold may yet buy us a ship." I let William puzzle at this for a moment.

"It is best to let them have the treasure," I said. "We'll damage one of their boats enough so that they leave it, but not so much as that we can't repair it." He nodded with understanding and I set him to the task.

"What are you doing?" he asked.

"Me? I'm going to make sure we survive the next few hours." I tucked the only dry and loaded pistol into my belt and led William off of the cliff.

Until now, the only trap I'd set was the one to catch the first croc. Although it may work on pirates as well, we didn't have the time to dig. I walked to the thick underbrush by the mouth of the cave and began tying the knives to the roots. When finished, I used leaves and branches to cover the knives from sight. The trap was crude, but it should slow them down.

William met me back at the mouth of the cave and we climbed back onto the overhang to watch where these pirates were headed. Four bodies, barely visible through the trees, made their way across the underbrush towards the spring. Then, their heads disappeared beneath the branches.

Several tense minutes passed before we heard them. We could tell how close they were by the screams. They howled and cursed as they drew nearer. Then one man's scream stopped all other noise.

"They found our traps," I told William. "There will be fewer, but they will be coming." A second man yelped in pain, still just out of our sight.

Two pirates emerged from the wood with pistols drawn. They looked back and shouted orders at the two injured men. William propped himself up higher to get a better view, but slipped on some rocks that cracked and splashed loudly below. One of the pirates, a stout red-haired Irishman, locked eyes with me from a distance and pointed with his sword.

William and I retreated into the cave. I tethered a row of hooks to a trigger on the end of a rope just over the mouth of the cave and drew the line in with me.

The sound of footfalls by the spring came as I predicted. I let the ones that weren't stopped by the knives get a six second head start toward the cave's entrance. I counted to William to ease his nerves. Three... Two... One... I let go and four hooks swung hard.

We heard two clangs. The rest hit meat and bone. Groans

filled the cave. William jumped and celebrated. I didn't have the heart to stop him. I readied my pistol.

"What are you doing?" he asked. I didn't need to answer. Slow grunts at the mouth of the cave told him all he needed to know. The stout Irishman climbed to his feet and faced us. He was younger than he looked. If I had to guess, I'd say he was no more than five years older than me.

It would be poor form to shoot an unarmed man. Fortunately, he had a pistol as well. We both aimed and fired. I felt wind brush past my ear. Mine went high to his left. He dropped it and drew a knife.

I was surprised he only had one pistol. In a way, I was upset. Being shot seemed a far quicker way to die than bleeding out from knife wounds.

William charged first, without thinking. The blades flashed wildly. The Irishman cut William's knife hand and drove the blade home through William's foot. I took this opportunity to attack, but the much stronger boy shoved me away. I landed against the rock wall. A jagged edge caught the side of my head. Thick blood oozed over my ear and the world blurred at the corners. Another thud and all went black.

Chapter Nineteen

Heat was on my face. There was light, but I could not see. Starbursts and flashes decorated an endless void behind my eyes. Someone was speaking. I tried to open my eyes but the pain of seeing was too much.

Cold, wet boards were beneath me. For a second, I thought that I was on my father's ship. Perhaps I fell overboard and had to be rescued. Pan, the battle, the island, and the pirates were all a dream.

However, no one on father's ship would kick me in the ribs after saving me from drowning. The fire in my side told me that I must be aboard the pirates' frigate. It told me something else, too. Pain told me that I lived.

"He stirs," the voice said.

My eyes cracked wide enough to see a toothless man standing over me. With him was the stout Irishman. Between them was the man-beast. He was tall, with black curls of hair from beneath his hat. His beard was slick and dark like an English night.

"What should we do with 'em?" the toothless man asked.

Them? The word snapped me to attention. Where was William? I found him, his cheeks stained with dried tears, at the feet of a fat and dirty pirate.

"Run them through," the Irishman responded. He dropped the four tethered hooks down at my feet. Two were bloodied. "We lost men."

"And where are they now?" said the man-beast. He sounded nearly human.

"All three are gone," the Irishman responded. "Only trails of blood remain." The answer slammed against me so fiercely that I couldn't help but speak.

"The croc," I breathed. The toothless man snatched me up by the back of my neck and hoisted me up to my feet.

"Keep yer mouth shut, boy," he said through the spaced black pearls in his mouth. He pulled a knife and tapped it menacingly against my cheek.

"Wait," the man-beast said. He looked down at me and we locked eyes. For a moment, he looked through me. "What did y' say?"

"The croc," I answered. "She lives on the island."

"Liars! Little English liars!" the Irishman shouted. "We saw no croc on the island." Other men shouted in agreement. The toothless one gripped my neck harder and turned my head toward whoever spoke.

"If there is no croc, then where did the men go?" the man-beast asked. His crew fell silent.

"The boys set traps..." the Irishman started.

"And these traps dragged the men away?" the black-bearded

captain asked. The Irishman seethed beneath his bright red skin. The man-beast took two broad steps as he questioned the crew. "Where are these traps now? Did anyone else see them?"

"Two parties landed after we 'eard shots, sir," the toothless one called out. "One boat was damaged, but we didn't see no traps."

"And the chest?"

"We got the chest," the toothless one smirked. His fractured grin shocked my memory once again. What happened to my father's belongings? With my toes, I gripped the coin that was still tucked away into my shoe. Sighing quietly, I slowly searched my pocket for my father's watch but found only cloth. My eyes searched frantically from pirate to pirate until they met the gaze of the stout Irishman, who patted his vest and sneered.

Again, the black-bearded man-beast looked through me to my very heart. He waited several painful moments before speaking.

"They will work," the man-beast finally said. The Irishman twisted where he stood. His face reddened further. The man-beast turned to meet his eyes. "That is my order, Smee, and I expect you to follow it."

"And the men we lost?" Smee shouted. His face was fully flush now with rage.

"If they were eaten by a mindless animal, then they were foolhardy and got what they deserved," the black- bearded man-beast said. "Spilling more blood won't replace my crew."

"This will be voted down," Smee barked.

"And so it will stand until then. What are your names, Little Englishmen?"

William answered quickly and honestly. "Billy Jukes." His words choked out in between panicked breaths. I'd never heard anyone call him "Billy" before, aside from his sister. I never asked whether he meant to use the name or if it was a reflex.

All eyes turned to me. If I were to be recognized as the son of a British captain, I might as well slit my own throat. My father was well known in the Caribbean, so I needed to look sharp.

"James…" A common enough name. Now I needed a last name to go with it. I looked frantically around the deck of the ship for a sign. My eyes rested on the blood stained steel at my knees. "…Hook."

James Hook. It wasn't the most inventive lie, mere letters off of my Christian name. Still, it was different enough that I was not recognized.

"Well, James Hook and Billy Jukes," the black-bearded one called out, "welcome to the *Queen Anne's Revenge.*"

Midday

Chapter Twenty

The *Jolly Roger* and her captor, the *Triumph*, rock in the violent waves of the passing storm. Dark clouds hide darker deeds as raging waters smash against each ship, muffling the sound of all crimes a man can commit. Deep within the hull of the *Triumph*, the imprisoned Captain James Hook recounts the tales of his life at the request of Admiral Charles Price.

The admiral is not impressed.

"At last, the point of this raving," Price says. He slumps back into his chair and slams his quill against the desk.

"Have I upset you?" Captain Hook asks.

"I've been wondering why you have taken me on this journey of falsehoods," the admiral snaps. He leans forward and allows venom to fill each word that escapes his wide face. "The feared Captain Hook is actually the poor marooned son of a respected captain in the Royal Navy, forced into piracy against his will." He chortles and clears his throat. "Neither your lies nor your lunacy will save you."

"You said you wanted to hear everything," Captain Hook chides with the upright posture of a diplomat. He tugs on the cuffs of his shirt, straightening any creases from the crewmen's earlier assault.

"Every detail of your piracy," Admiral Price says through clenched teeth, "specifically the events of Port Royal and how you got control of the *Jolly Roger*."

"I was just getting to that, Admiral," Hook says with a smile. "You have hardly given me a chance and I do get off track without my watch." Captain Hook points to the gold watch that Admiral Price is currently fiddling with between his thick fingers. Price clenches it tightly and shoves it into his jacket pocket.

A strong wind rocks the ship hard to the left. "It seems that the admiral is not going to be generous with my watch, gentlemen," Hook says to the crewmen on either side of the admiral. "Would you happen to know how much longer this storm will last?"

The larger one just scowls and shakes his head at Hook. The shorter crewman, hair graying on the sides, leans in toward the admiral and says, "We're not clear yet, sir. This one's lasting longer than we thought."

"In that case, Admiral," Hook offers, "allow me to entertain you further. We do seem to have nothing but time."

"How much longer is this tall tale of yours going to be?" Price asks while unfurling a new roll of parchment.

"Don't worry, Admiral. The end comes sooner than you think."

The Tale of Piracy

Chapter Twenty-One

In the days that followed, all but Smee grew tired of hitting me. He took extra long to "make up for what the boys are missing out on." My body scabbed over and endured. William hardened slower than I did. He wept often for his father or sister. I knew enough to keep my mouth shut. The beatings only got worse when you cried.

Every child thinks he knows the world. I fooled myself into believing I could escape a pirate ship. I looked out to islands that were within swimming distance and tested lifeboats. Opportunity never came, but I was patient. I whispered to William that we would find a way back home. I told him that pirates were stupid and nothing could shake our resolve.

I was taught a humbling lesson the day we took the French cruiser.

Smee spotted it at a distance. The toothless one knew the style of ship and its country of origin. The black-bearded captain gave the order. The savages scrambled to hoist French flags all over the ship. We pulled our guns back and crept slowly to our prey. The plan was ingenious in its deception.

William and I were hurried downstairs to ready the gunpowder. Smee followed to make sure we did as we were told. As an Englishman, I had no love for the French. Still, I'd rather be with them than pirates. At least I could have been ransomed or bargained for like a civilized human being.

Most of the pirates hid below deck. From where I stood, I could see the fat one at the top of the ladder. He waved at the oncoming ship like an old friend while wearing a stolen French uniform. The fools approached without caution. I watched them through a porthole as they stood on their deck, waving in return.

Blackbeard was below deck with us. He sat in the dark corners of the cabin and tied candles into the thick tendrils of his obsidian beard. When the first sounds of battle hit our ears, he lit them and became fully the man-beast of children's nightmares. Acrid sulfur stung our noses as he passed us to climb on deck and join the fray.

The fight was quick and merciless. Long guns split masts. The shorter barreled cannons punched man-sized holes in the flank of the ship. Grappling hooks were cast over and a boarding party swarmed their deck, cutting and spitting. It was over within minutes.

Almost.

"Your turn, ladies," Smee said as he yanked William and me to our feet and onto the deck. Two French sailors lay face down, badly beaten. Smee shoved a pistol in each of our hands.

William fired his immediately and dropped his pistol. The sailor on the left cried out once and was silent. William curled into a ball behind the barrel of grain, whimpering softly.

"Last but not least," the fat one said into my ear. Smee pointed a knife in my back. Even if I were to shoot the fat one or the toothless pirate, I wouldn't live another minute. I had to keep my promise and get William home.

Blackbeard watched from the deck of the French ship. My shame grew as others stopped loading supplies to watch with amusement.

The Frenchman, now on his knees, begged for his life. In any language, begging always sounded the same. I squeezed my eyes shut and pulled the trigger. Acrid smoke kicked up in my face and I coughed as the toothless pirate turned my head. His fingers pulled my eyelids open so I could watch.

The Frenchman convulsed on the floorboards. His uniform was spattered with red from his chest. He coughed and more blood came. I didn't understand what he was saying, but he didn't talk for long.

The man's eyes dimmed and he was gone.

The beatings stopped entirely after that. Toothless grins and pats on the back were all I got from that moment forward from my new family. Something inside me spoiled as I realized that there was no going home without bringing something unwanted home with me.

Chapter Twenty-Two

The weeks that William and I spent aboard the *Queen Anne's Revenge* melted into months. When we weren't running messages between Blackbeard and his crew, we swabbed the deck, prepared food for the cook, and rigged the chain and bundle shots for the cannons before battle. It was hard work, but we dared not complain. William Howard was a stern Quartermaster and Smee, the ship's Boatswain, was ever-watching for a reason to "toughen us up some."

One morning, I was by the main mast hitching the sheets when I overheard Blackbeard squabbling with the other animals. Smee held a crumpled map and stared off into the horizon. Next to him was Stede Bonnet, a tall and soft-spoken and, as far as I could tell, well-educated scoundrel. Not long before William and I were taken onto the *Queen Anne's Revenge*, Bonnet's crew became Blackbeard's crew and he became little more than a guest on the ship. As they got louder with each other, I split my effort between working the knots and listening in on the argument.

"You don't know what yer saying," Blackbeard bellowed as he ripped the charts from Smee's hands. "You'd have us dead in two days." I didn't know whether it was Blackbeard's tone or the animated way he tore the charts from his crewmate's grip, but I let out a slight chuckle. It wasn't much, but it was loud enough. I tried to reach out and pull the sounds of my laughter back into me, but I failed and found myself the focus of their hardened stares. My blood froze as I looked into Blackbeard's red, sunken eyes.

"You want to try, Little Englishman?" he asked. Although it was worded like an offer, there was an edge of challenge to his tone. I'd always been very good with charts, but I didn't know what sort of answer he was expecting. Would he be angrier if I said "yes" and thought I could do better than his crewmate or if I said "no" and shrank further into my skin? My next move may decide whether I continued breathing and I must live. Emily and my mother were waiting for our safe return and Heath Ashley and Jesse Labette were waiting for my bloody revenge. These men stood between me and what was just and, frankly, I was tired of shrinking.

I rose to my feet and walked over to them. Blackbeard shoved the charts in my hands and the three of them stood over me like ogres.

"Well, boy," Blackbeard grumbled, "we're headed through these patches of islands here." He pointed to where the ship was on the map and then again quickly at where we were headed. "How would you get us killed?"

Part of me hoped that I'd at least see Port Royal nearby, but we were far too many miles southeast. Port Royal wasn't even on this map. The second thing I noticed was that our heading led out deep into the ocean and stopped at nothing. No island. No port. Only open sea for miles outside of Rio.

"There's nothing out there," I started. Smee went to take the map from my hands but Blackbeard stopped him with an arm across the chest.

"Don't you mind where we're going," he said. "Just get us there in one piece." The challenging tone rose in his voice again and I knew I had to try.

I nodded, took a deep breath, and got to work. My time memorizing father's charts helped guide me as I began by carving a path around areas I knew the English and Spanish ships would be. Even though I would have loved to be taken in by a Royal Navy ship, I couldn't bare the idea of the *Queen Anne's Revenge* taking any English lives. I drew my route quickly, taking into account tides, currents, and seasonal winds. When finished, I looked up at them proudly.

"Seven days," I told them. "Four if we sail at full through the night." I handed Blackbeard the charts and he began looking them over. Smee's face flushed red and he stormed below deck while Stede just blinked dimly. I turned to Blackbeard and said, "But I wouldn't suggest sailing at night since the islands are so close together…"

"We'd be dead on day five," Blackbeard croaked. He lowered the chart down to his side and looked me dead in the eye. "Day three if we 'sail at full.'"

"But that's not possible," I argued. I had always prided myself on my skills in mathematics. There was no way that I could have been wrong.

"Not possible, is it?" Blackbeard said through squinted eyes. "And yer confident that you've thought of everything, are ya?" I opened my mouth to defend my numbers, but he cut me off before I could utter a sound.

"Have you any idea how deep the bilge is on this ship, boy?" Blackbeard continued. "How about how much she weighs with a full crew aboard?" I looked at the chart stupidly, knowing that I didn't have an answer.

"She'll be sunk here," he pointed to a spot on the chart between two widely spaced islands, "where the coral reaches high enough to tear holes the size of men into the hull."

After seeing that I understood, he leaned in and gave me this warning. "Above all else, know yer ship, Mr. Hook. Know her well." I nodded as the reason behind this task finally became clear to me. This wasn't a threat or a punishment. It was a lesson. But why would he take the time to teach me anything? Weren't these animals just going to kill us when we've outlasted our use?

William and I worked day and night, but since that morning, it seemed we hardly saw one another at all. Blackbeard took more and more of my time, teaching me charts, strategy, and currency, while William spent nearly every day sweating above deck under Smee's watchful glare.

We passed while working, to be sure, but gone were the days of long talks about returning home. In the brief moments I saw William, I looked into his eyes and feared that all hope had left him. Worse, I feared that he saw the same in me.

Chapter Twenty-Three

We traveled the route Blackbeard charted and, on the day we arrived, I saw the ghost of the *Britannia*. Her tall, piercing masts were unmistakable, even at a distance. For long minutes, the world around me blurred and the only thing that existed was that one dark stain on an otherwise calm blue sea.

Thousands of thoughts ran through my mind at once. Had my father's death been a dream? Had I gone overboard and washed up on the island only to imagine burying him? Had he come to rescue me from these monsters who now greeted me with smiles? My toes gripped the coin in my shoe, telling me the truth of what had happened.

My father was dead.

There was no rescue.

Jesse Labette captained the *Britannia*.

As the ship drew nearer, I saw more evidence of this horrid truth. The king's colors were gone. Even the name, *Britannia*, had been scraped off of her hull. Thick blood churned in my veins as my eyes fixed on the ship-killer known as Long Tom, the two-ton cannon that wiped my father from this Earth. It grew larger as it approached, stalking me, searching for me, looking to finish the job it started years ago. She was the *Jolly Roger* now. But how?

"My god," I breathed after long moments without air. Time started again and I began to see and feel the world around me. I was at one of the port holes in the Blackbeard's cabin, close enough to the man-beast for him to have heard me. Blackbeard rose from his chair and trudged over to the window to my right.

"He's late," he said. His breaths were slow and measured as he turned to me. "Join the men on deck."

"For battle?" I asked, grabbing a knife.

"No, Mr. Hook," Blackbeard said. I stopped just short of the door and turned back to meet his red, puffy eyes. "For a trade."

"Trade?" I repeated foolishly. What trade could there be with a fiend such as Jesse Labette? He was a killer of men and, along with Heath Ashley the betrayer, the reason I was not at home with my mother and Emily. I stammered more sounds together before speaking again in a way that could be understood. "What for?"

"Her captain is partial to louis-d'ors," Blackbeard grumbled. He went on to explain that the French cruiser we took held a good amount of their native currency, a favorite of Jesse Labette. That, combined with the chest that was recovered from the island, made for a weighty sum. It seemed that the *Queen Anne's Revenge* was in need of supplies that the new *Jolly Roger* had in surplus.

"Yer good with numbers, aren't ya boy?" Blackbeard said. I nodded, still not sure what role I had to play in this and how my situation could get any worse. Then Blackbeard showed me that there was no limit to my misfortune. "Good, you and Smee are with me."

Blackbeard split his crew into three groups. William Howard

manned the helm with three armed men at his back and another fifteen hiding pistols under loose clothes while "working" the ship's daily maintenance. Stede Bonnet paced at the fore of the ship with a second armed grouping of men, some of which he kept loyal with his purse. William stayed below deck with the third group who readied the cannons and themselves against any sounds of betrayal. I was on the deck at the right hand of Blackbeard, with Smee on his left.

We stood in silence as the *Jolly Roger* crept up alongside us. She was shorter and narrower than this frigate, but she was a heavily armed brigantine and carried Long Tom. If we were to go to battle at this range, neither ship would survive. Fighting would have to be done crew to crew and we had more hands. He'd have to be a fool to take us on.

The men on deck tethered lines to hooks and cast them onto the *Jolly Roger*. They drew the ships closer to one another and extended planks across each deck. The crew of the brigantine hailed us with smiles and cheers of greeting. Throughout this, Blackbeard remained steady, watching each man's movement.

Three men stepped across the plank from the *Jolly Roger*. As each one passed, I realized that I had no idea what Jesse Labette looked like. Someone so vile had to have a telling appearance. I watched them closely for signs of monstrous horror, but not one had a tail, horns, or an inhuman glow in their eyes. The three of them lined up, demons in men's clothing. The one in the middle stepped forward and bowed. The monster by my side spoke first.

"Welcome aboard the *Queen Anne's Revenge*, Captain Labette," Blackbeard said, returning the pirate's bow with a nod. The pirate rose and removed his wide-brimmed black hat, revealing long hair that was tightly pulled back. Its color was fair against his face, which was dark and dry from years at sea.

"'Tis good to be welcomed," the pirate grinned.

A thousand thoughts came to me at once. Although he answered to the name, this man could not be Jesse Labette, the feared killer of honorable men. He was no taller than any other man and despite the bulk of his coat, he was no broader either. What if my mother was right and these pirates were only men and nothing more? Blackbeard was certainly a savage, but he was no troll or beast. If he was a man, then Jesse Labette was as well. A man can be betrayed. A man can be killed. Blood pounded heavily in my ears and a red cloud crept in around the edges of my vision. Buried in his chest beat a heart blacker than a moonless night and I wanted to tear it from his corpse with my own two hands.

Blackbeard stepped forward and motioned for Labette to follow, which he did. Blackbeard chose Smee to talk this trade over with Labette in the captain's cabin. My job was to wait outside until I was needed to count the money and I assumed Labette's third crewman was charged with the same task.

They walked shoulder to shoulder exchanging tense smiles as I strained to hold myself still. If I lunged for Labette now, I'd surely be killed. Here, surrounded by his friends and Blackbeard's crew, was not the place. Today, I told myself, I am not prepared to win. I stopped at the door and watched Jesse Labette, the murderer of my future, close the door behind him.

Chapter Twenty-Four

Blackbeard's negotiations with Jesse Labette took over three hours. Coarse talk was punctuated with shouts, threats, and laughter. It was impossible to hear fully what was being discussed, but large sums of money were at stake.

My task in this trade was to guard the door until I was told how many louis-d'ors to count out. Waiting wasn't a difficult job, save for the company. One of the pirates that came over with Jesse Labette was outside the cabin with me and reeked like brine, which appeared to be crusted into his beard. An evening wind picked up, and I wondered if I smelled any better.

The noise inside the cabin died down to a whisper seconds before the door burst open.

"You're up," Smee barked at us. Stunned to alertness, I locked eyes with the crusty-bearded pirate, who already had his hand on the pistol in his belt. He smiled and laughed to himself, shaking salt from his beard onto the deck. Smee leered at him before adding, "Come on, then."

The two of us entered and Smee closed the door behind him, sealing me in with my nightmares. The two captains sat facing one another on either side of the dark table that Blackbeard used for business and dining. Jesse Labette laughed heartily as Blackbeard toasted the agreement. Both men drank while Smee smiled through a scowl at Labette's pirates, who sneered back at him.

"Mr. Hook," Blackbeard said, finally noticing me. "This is Captain Labette."

"Yes, sir, I know," I said out of reflex. Labette perked the corner of his mouth into a smirk and tilted his head in curiosity. I looked at the floor, purposely avoiding his gaze. Earlier, I resolved to keep my temper at bay. One slip here and William and I would never see home again.

Then Labette leaned forward and asked, "Have we met, Mr. Hook?"

"No, sir," I said, meeting his eyes for the first time. "I'd only heard of you up until now." He rested his back against the chair with a wide self-satisfied grin across his face. His eyes remained fixed on me, as if he were examining me. Blackbeard roared with laughter and raised his glass to toast their notoriety. When he set the glass back on the table, I asked him, "What do I need to count, sir?"

"No counting," Blackbeard said. "Captain Labette just wanted to get a good look at ya is all, being that you'll be carrying the chests." Smee snorted at me and grinned. Blackbeard waved his arm over the two chests behind his chair. "These are his." Questions formed in my mind, but instead I nodded and lifted one of the chests. The sooner I was out of this cabin and away from Labette, the better. I got halfway through the door when Blackbeard dashed my hopes of escape.

"You and Smee'll be taking these chests over to the *Jolly Roger*." My heart and stomach changed places for an instant. The

Jolly Roger? I could barely look at the ship without flying into a rage. I stifled my panic long enough to catch Labette still watching my every move. I managed to breathe an, "Aye, sir," before leaving.

A strong gust caught me as I stepped onto the deck, but that wasn't what chilled me. The *Jolly Roger* creaked and snarled as the wind cut through her sails. I steeled myself before crossing the plank that connected the two ships.

As I stepped onto the dark ship, her crew watched me out of the sides of their eyes. They were split in much the same way as ours. Men were here and about, pretending to work while armed to the teeth. They cackled and joked to themselves just before I was hit.

Something hard slammed into my back and I tumbled forward, spilling the chest in my hands. It crashed and sprang open with a bang. Coins leapt from within and scattered like mice behind the corner where Emily kissed me those years ago. The men fell silent. Some drew weapons. I crawled on my knees to gather the money back into the chest.

"Look sharp," Smee snickered loudly. He took a few steps and placed the chest down on the deck before turning to sneer again. He flicked open my father's watch and looked at it briefly before speaking again. "You'd better clean up your mess, Hook."

"No," was all I said at first. If the ships were quiet before I spoke, they were a cemetery now. "This mess is yours and that watch is mine."

Smee flushed red and looked about him at the hushed, dirty faces. "It is a pretty watch, Hook, but it is mine."

"When we're all laid low," I said, "we'll see who's laid with it." Smee took two steps toward me and I rushed to greet him. Up until this point, I hadn't realized how much I'd grown in my time away. I was almost eye to eye with him.

"If you're going to stab me, then do it." I challenged. "No? How about shooting me?" All the time that I'd spent cowering was over. There would be no more fear.

Smee paused and then paced around me, snorting like an animal. He stopped, pulled the knife from his belt, and dropped it to the floor with a thud. His fists clenched in that most familiar preamble to my beating.

"Ahoy, Little Floater!" called a voice from a distance. The blood drained from Smee's face as he and I both looked to the *Queen Anne's Revenge*. Calling out again, Jesse Labette sauntered across the plank. "You handle yourself well, Smee," he said. "You spend a few years on a ship and now you're running trade agreements with the captain and ordering the boys around on deck." Smee met his eyes with a murderous rage. Labette strode up to him grinning like the devil himself. "You've come a long way from the board we found you floating on."

The color returned to Smee's face as he pulsed with anger. They stared at each other for moments before Labette spoke again. It wasn't a long pause, but I had time to wonder. What happens when one beast swallows another? Does he grow stronger for the victory or is he less of what he was from the fight?

"Mr. Hook," Labette said to me without once looking my way, "have you ever heard how Smee came aboard the *Queen Anne's Revenge*? Or how he got his name?"

"No," I answered. Although I wanted to know, I'd rather find a safe distance from the both of them.

"Back when I served as Boatswain under Blackbeard, months after we first took the ship, we saw this tubby Irish boy floating on a board in the open sea," Labette said. He squinted a little and pulled the corner of his mouth into a smirk. "For the life of me,

I have no idea why we didn't just let him drift. He had no valuables and he'd been stabbed through the gullet." Smee brought a hand to his stomach, much to Labette's amusement.

"But dragged him up we did and we laid him across the deck and we listened. For although he was so near death, he kept saying the same thing over and over again, 'Smee,' 'Smee,' 'Smee.'" Labette smiled even more broadly now. "Even when he'd healed enough for us to be certain that he'd live, he kept saying that word, 'Smee,' 'Smee,' 'Smee.'" Since I was sure now that no one was watching me, I tried to slink away. Labette shot me a hard look, freezing me in place.

"Soon," he continued. "He was strong enough to talk so we asked him what 'Smee' meant. The part that slays me to this day was that he didn't know." The men listening in on the *Jolly Roger* laughed heartily. "He had no memory save for his time with us on the ship. No history. No name. So we called him 'Smee, the Little Floater.'" At this, several aboard the *Revenge* joined in the mocking as well.

Smee, reddened in his humiliation, stormed over to the *Revenge*.

"Go and run off, Smee," Labette chided. "Run off before I give you ol' Johnny Corkscrew." He took out a sword and twisted it in the air in a mock stabbing motion, laughing horribly. The crewmates who took part of the teasing ceased immediately when Smee got back aboard. I tried to follow quietly, but Labette blocked my passage.

"And where are you going, Mr. Hook?" he asked. I opened my mouth to speak, but the dozens of questions I had caught in my throat. How did he get my father's ship? What did he do to the men still aboard? Where was the ship he once had? My mind raced until I saw an oddly familiar sight. Although Labette smiled often, he did so with everything except his eyes. It's a look I recognized, but still didn't understand.

"You've still got a mess to clean up," Labette told me, pointing to the spilled coins. He spun on his heels and strode to my father's cabin. Before he disappeared into the room, he called out over his shoulder, "And be sure to count out the right amount before you leave."

The long minutes I spent picking the louis-d'ors up off of the deck of the *Jolly Roger* stretched to nearly an hour. I tallied the total twice to be sure that each coin was accounted for. When finished, I bolted back to the *Revenge*. I sat below deck for an hour before my heart beat normally again.

The final exchanges were made in the fading light of dusk. Both crews relaxed their hardened looks and began the celebration. Although drunkenness is not generally allowed on board, the men told tales of their adventures with as much bluster as possible. I did my best to join in, but there was only so much bragging I could stand, especially from Labette, who was now recounting his narrow escape from a tribe of savage cannibals.

As the men laughed and joked, I slipped away to the aft deck and hung my legs over the side. The moon was so very full and bright that I could not look at it without wondering if Emily was watching it as well. I was hundreds of miles away from home, surrounded by murderous liars and cheats, yet this moon was the same one over Port Royal tonight.

At that moment, I heard footsteps approach. They weren't the pace of a man or a child, but someone in between. Without looking, I asked William the first thought on my mind.

"What could fate have in store for us next?" The footsteps stopped for a moment. I didn't expect William to answer this question, but what happened next defied expectation.

"I wouldn't know," replied a voice that wasn't William's. I

turned and saw a boy, tall and broad, with a head the size and color of a ham. He grinned broadly and added, "but I hope it's a good time."

"And you are?" I asked. He began boasting before I drew breath to speak again.

"I go by a great many names, to be sure," the boy said. "Some call me the Sea-Cook." He leapt up onto a barrel and drew his sword. "Others call me Barbeque." He cut at the air with delicate ease, then jumped down, jabbed the sword into the deck and met my eyes for the first time. "But for the purpose of introduction, you may call me John Silver."

Chapter Twenty-Five

Surrounded by thieves and murderers, it was foolish to let my guard down for long. I seldom slept and I almost never stared at the stars anymore. On a night like this, when the moon was so bright that Emily must have been watching it as well, I should have been enjoying my moment of solitude. Instead, I was forced to deal with a young braggart from the *Jolly Roger* by the name of John Silver.

"Even as young as I am, most of the men fear me," he said, puffing out his chest. "Do you know why?" He spoke non-stop since he first walked up and I was desperate to quiet him. Ignoring him didn't seem to work, so I decided to try insults.

"They're afraid you'd talk them to death?" I told him. His jaw tightened slightly, but he continued unabated.

"It's 'cause I'm big for my age," he said. He was right, too. Despite being younger than I was, he stood a full head taller than I did. He grinned broadly and posed, "They know I'll get bigger than 'em all in a year or two, so they leave me alone." He looked me over before snidely adding, "You're not so big though, are ya?"

There were only so many more slights that I could stand. If ignoring him didn't work and insults only got me insulted in return, what could I do to get rid of him? Maybe he needed to see how small he really was.

"You're the son of the cook on the *Jolly Roger*," I said in a way that told him I was not asking. Wisps of rage fluttered across his face.

"Ya seem t'know your share of other people's business," he said through his teeth. He wouldn't expect me to know much about him, or anyone else aboard the *Jolly Roger*, for that matter. Truth be told, I knew very little before the ship arrived, but I was a quick study.

"I ask a lot of questions," I told him. His eyes narrowed as he examined me a second time.

"And you talk like a Royal," he said.

"I read a lot," I shot back. "You should try it sometime."

"T'be sure," he said. "And what is your name, Royal?"

"James Hook."

"I have t'know, James Hook," John Silver said. "Do you make it a habit of getting in the middle of a fight between a captain and the officers?" The question staggered me for a moment. I was ashamed to admit that I didn't know where his ceaseless talking was leading. He must have seen the stand-off between Smee and Jesse Labette and now wanted to know my role in it. It seemed that John Silver wasn't as mindless as he let on.

"They wouldn't have fought," I said.

"Is that so?"

"It's code," I told him. "Any quarrel between the men has to take place on land away from the ship."

"Well then," he snorted, "if it is code then it must be honored at all times." He let out a laugh that shook his coat then chuckled to himself for a few more minutes. Several times, he drew breath to speak again, but decided not to. Finally, he walked over to the railing, picked up his sword, and said, "How about some exercise?"

"We can't fight on the ship," I reminded him.

"Who's fighting?" he asked, feigning innocence. "I just want a little practice." He cracked a wry smile and stood at guard. No matter what he called it, it was clear that this practice, like the entire conversation before it, was more that it seemed.

I drew my sword and, instantly, I was met with a quick thrust that sliced the side of my shirt. Furious, I began to call him a madman, but before I could speak the word, I was met with a second thrust that sliced the other side of my shirt.

"One move is all I need to end you," Silver said. "You hesitate. I can kill any man with hesitation in his eyes." He thrust again, but this time I jumped back and got a good look at his technique. Before he moves, he measures the distance between him and his target. Then he steps hard with his lead foot and drives the sword in a straight line with the whole weight of his body behind it.

"That's an impressive thrust," I told him.

"I fight a lot," he swiped. "You should try it sometime." With his arm raised, he stepped heavy with his lead foot. Steel clashed loudly in the night as I blocked his attack. Harrison Jukes, William's father and first officer to my father, taught me a great many things about evading a stronger opponent.

"I handle my own fights," I countered.

"Of course you do," he said. Again he thrust and again I dodged and parried as Mr. Jukes taught me years ago. "You can plan and think your whole life and get nowhere," Silver told me. "Action is the only thing that these men respect."

He swiped low and pivoted to thrust. I knew that if I let him follow through on this attack, he could drive the point of his sword through my heart. I also knew that once he started moving forward, he could only go one direction. I led his sword away to the right and tripped him to the left, sending him crashing against the railing. He regained his footing quickly and snapped around to face me.

"I'll kill you for that!" he spat. His face reddened and his eyes narrowed to the point of almost closing. I didn't expect him to like the fall he took, but nothing could have prepared me for this reaction. A man as proud as John Silver couldn't have a moment of embarrassment, even a private one, at the hands of someone he sees as weak.

He charged at me with his sword raised and howled. He swung wildly over my head before swiping downward to cut me in half. Realizing that I could not keep fighting at this pace with my condition, I parried, turned, and ran my blade across the top of his hand, drawing blood. He hissed and dropped the weapon onto the deck.

His rage-filled eyes met mine, but he refused to admit defeat. A dark thought hardened his wide face as he drove his forehead into the bridge of my nose and kicked me to the floorboards. "No one does that to me!" he said as he stomped over to his fallen sword.

But as John Silver bent down to grab the hilt, a large foot stepped on the flat of the blade. He tried to yank the sword out from under the large-footed person, but even in his rage he couldn't budge the weapon. Furious, he stood tall and looked up into the eyes of William.

For a moment, I didn't realize that this hulking figure was William. After knowing him for as long as I had, I had a picture in my mind of what he should look like. He was nearly as tall as his father now and almost as broad. He shot John Silver a look that chilled the air.

William and Silver stared daggers at one another for seconds. From the floor, I watched these two giants silently dare the other to make a first move. Neither man backed down. Neither man talked. Then William, slowly at first, raised a freshly tattooed arm and shoved Silver back several steps.

"Go back to your ship like a good Sea Dog," William grunted. Of the hopes I'd held onto, one I'd cherished most was the idea that William would remain as unchanged throughout our journey home as I have been. It seemed now that that hope was dead.

John Silver took a heavy step forward, but stopped short of where he stood before. William refused to move.

"My sword," Silver said.

"Aren't you coming for it?" William asked. Silver snorted as he looked from William to me and back again.

"More of you handling your own fights, eh James?" John Silver teased.

"His fights ARE my fights," William snarled.

John Silver nodded at that and turned to walk back to the lower deck, but before his heavy footfalls faded into the sounds of the night, he said, "Funny thing 'bout Smee is that his fight wasn't with Captain Labette." His smile was broad again and his face was no longer flush with frustration. "The fight with Smee is yours, and he won't change until you do."

His words ran through my mind in the next few hours. John Silver, a boy William's age, had to show me how much more he knew about surviving as a pirate than I did. He not only taught me that critical thrust, but he also showed me that action, tempered with patience, was the better part of luck. Smee would not let up on me until he was dead or soundly defeated. Either one took time.

That night, I watched the dark ship pull away and wondered what kind of coward I was. Not only had Smee and John Silver gotten the better of me today, but Jesse Labette was within my grasp and I let him slip.

As the *Jolly Roger* disappeared into the darkness, I breathed deeply and promised my seething hatred delayed satisfaction.

Chapter Twenty-Six

In the spring, we seized the sloop *Adventure* and the ship *Protestant Caesar* in the Bay of Honduras. William Howard and Smee captained these ships. I stayed on the *Queen Anne's Revenge* as Boatswain. It was more responsibility than I was used to, but I learned quickly.

Thanks in part to the time I spent with William's father, Mr. Jukes, I developed a guilty sense of pride in my work. Maintenance mostly. The *Revenge* was a big ship to keep up: three masts and forty guns. I was good with numbers, so when I told Blackbeard that we'd run out of supplies in three days, he could be sure I had it rationed down to the hour.

When we sailed into sight of Charles Town, no one on shore panicked at first. We raised no colors, nor fired any cannons. Only after we captured our first ship and added it to our flotilla did the dock erupt in wails of terror and helplessness.

I was not let in on why we were blockading the port at first. I figured the usual gold, silver, and supplies. With three ships, we had the cargo space to feed the men for weeks after our departure. Only when a landing party was being gathered with a list of demands, did I learn the truth.

Several of Blackbeard's men had become ill with the Foul disease. I'd heard it called the French Disease by my father's men. I learned from my shipmates that the French called it the Italian disease and the Italians had a name for it that reddened the cheeks of hardened sailors. As for Blackbeard, himself, I'd never check his britches, but he was as motivated as any man to get these medicines.

William went with the landing party. The fat pirate had taken him under his wing since William was sent to work on the *Adventure* under Captain Smee. In the one glance I got of him, I saw how little there was left of the boy I swore to protect behind those eyes. He sang a song with the landing party as they rowed to shore.

"Yo ho, yo ho, the pirates' song,
So bright, so fierce, so bold.
Onward we press to distant lands,
Our thoughts and spirits cold."

The dreadful song built in volume as the other pirates joined in with smiles and hoarse voices.

"Belay the talk and promises,
Of treasures yet to hold.
Our only prize is servitude,
To whom our souls are sold."

We added more ships to the flotilla as they unwittingly drifted into port. One by one, they all surrendered and were boarded. No one fought. The merchant ships had the more common treasures you would come to expect. The *Crowley* was the payload. Mostly men, but some women and children. These were the families of a wealthier class, the type of citizen who would pay any ransom to see to a safe return.

"Get down to the cargo hold an' strip it of anythin' useful," the toothless one ordered. "We're goin' for the passengers."

The manifest read that this ship was carrying supplies from a larger port up north. The stores aboard were standard, save for one corner. In a chest underneath several sacks of grain was a collection of drafts and potions. None of them were the mercury salves, ointment, and tincture of mercury that were needed from the town, but they were interesting nonetheless. I spent an hour reading and comparing the labels. I took one vial and emptied the contents onto the floorboards. Into it, I poured a lethal combination of arsenic, strychnine, and cyanide. Under the best circumstances, I could quietly dispose of an unwanted foe. As a last resort, I could prevent myself the indignity of a hanging.

While the landing party went ashore to negotiate, I was left in charge of guarding some of the prisoners. It was during one such duty that a young man approached the bars.

"James?" he asked. I was instantly frozen. "James, what are you doing?"

He was Thomas Darling, one of William's former classmates at Port Royal. I didn't recognize him at first, but it was definitely Thomas. If I was a foolish man, I would have embraced an old friend, exposed my identity, and surely be killed for my lineage. Instead, I played this one much closer to the chest.

"I can't talk now, Thomas," I said. "We don't intend to kill anyone. Stay quiet and I'll talk to you after the next guard change when I'm alone."

From the porthole, I saw the supply of medicines being loaded onto the ships. Realizing I didn't have another shift to wait, I relied on my wits. A plan formed.

"Thomas, you need to write a letter to my mother and tell her what has happened to me. Draft a letter for her and also write one to Emily Jukes. I am giving you specific information. You need to remember this exactly as I tell it to you..."

Weeks passed. Many of the men slept fitfully, wrapped in salves and heavy blankets. The hacking and sweating and drooling that were part of the purging of the Foul disease didn't disturb my sleep. I was awake, counting and recounting. I needed to tell Blackbeard how long we had until we were forced to risk another siege. Only days remained and I was tired of waiting for luck or providence.

Chapter Twenty-Seven

The *Queen Anne's Revenge* ran aground in the Topsail Inlet of Fish Town, just as I had planned. I'd always been really good with charts and the bilge of the ship was very deep, after all. Since I had proven myself superior in the calculation of supplies, Blackbeard didn't doubt me for a second that it was time for a siege in the precise spot I'd told Thomas Darling we'd be weeks earlier. Blackbeard was usually much sharper, but he'd spent so many of these days in bed rest due to the medicines he'd been taking that he would not have doubted me one way or the other.

I expected a brief exchange and our capture as a crew. It would have been the civilized way to surrender. At that point, William and I could have revealed our identities and chartered a ship back to Port Royal. Never did I think that Blackbeard would cut a deal for himself and his closest friends, leaving the rest of us to scramble. In the chase, I didn't risk stopping to explain my situation. I would likely have been called a liar and shot on the spot. So, instead, William and I ran for our lives.

After a brief sprint down two alleys it became clear that I couldn't keep this pace up for much longer. My condition didn't allow for too much excited movement. We dove into a tavern and found a table in the corner. We were too young to be in here, but the place was dark enough. We hid there for a moment and tried to not draw attention to ourselves.

"We can't stay," I told William. "We have to get ready to leave soon, and not in a way that will get us noticed." I began planning, but I was interrupted by one of William's random thoughts.

"Maybe we should," he said.

"Maybe we should, what?" I said by reflex. I didn't usually give his comments much thought and I didn't intend to start.

"Stay," William said. "Maybe we should stay."

"We can't stay in the tavern," I told him. "We'll be found out."

"I don't mean that we should stay in the tavern, James," he said. "I just think that maybe we should stay and, you know, … not go home."

If words were fists, then William would have just laid me out on the floor. How could he not want to go home? What had this whole experience been about if not for the prize of returning to Port Royal?

"Besides," he trailed off, "after what we did…" His eyes got distant and it hit me. William wasn't easily forgetting the time on the *Queen Anne's Revenge*, especially the seizing of the French cruiser and the murder of her crew. It was something that had been bothering him for some time. I wasn't sure whether I should have felt sorrier for him, or sorrier for me in that I hadn't thought about it in weeks.

"No," I told him. "You're safe, but that's only half the job. We get home to our families." I remembered what he said and added, "They'll understand." I almost believed it, too. I knew I could hide nearly anything from my mother, but Emily saw right through me. I thought of a dozen ways I could tell Emily. Each of them ended with her understanding, but never really liking it or ever looking at me the same. Just like when I told her about Pan.

Just then, a quarrel at one of the tables spilled out onto the bar. I craned my neck to see over the man in front of me. I was surprised to see a familiar face, even one I'd never hoped to see again. It appeared Smee got here ahead of us and had already begun making friends. I didn't know what he said, but it seemed to have upset half of the tavern.

"That sloop is ours for the taking," said a formally dressed man. Smee was then grabbed by two of the others.

As strong as Smee was, the odds were six to one. The Italian and a man with backwards hands were working him over as I walked up. The clean-cut gentleman drew his sword and raised it to thrusting height, his wrist bent at an awkwardly dainty angle. Poor form. I was tempted to wait until Smee was run through, but I decided better of it. He was a strong and crafty sailor. The devil you know always wins out.

"Stop!" I shouted. "Do you know who this man is? That's Smee, cutthroat and scourge of the Caribbean." I only wanted their attention, but my voice quieted the entire tavern. The gentleman looked William and me over before speaking.

"What's he worth to you?" the gentleman asked.

"To me, nothing. He's worth an untold amount to you though. You're about to stab the one man who knows of the location of Blackbeard's buried treasure." It was a flimsy lie. Still, it was the best I could come up with in the heat of confrontation.

"That's rich coming from Blackbeard's own Bos'n," Smee added, obviously catching on to my plan.

"What about him?" the gentleman asked, pointing his sword at William.

"Bill Jukes," I cried out, "A tattoo for every kill since the raid of Charles Town." More quick thinking.

"You're all from the ship that ran aground?" the Gentleman responded. "Maybe we'll turn you three in for a generous reward?"

"And turn yourselves in as well?" I shot back. One look at their clothes told the whole tale. Most of them were clearly stolen. The Italian was wearing the shirt of a British soldier. Hardened men shrank from sight and scattered like rats. Several practiced killers exited the tavern in the moments before I spoke again. "I doubt it. I know wanted men when I see them."

"Then we'll kill the two of you and torture the information out of your friend here," he said. I liked him instantly. He was a thinker. Even so, he was one step behind.

"You don't have enough time for that," I told him. "Remember, we're being hunted. A sloop is a complicated ship. She'll need an experienced crew of more men than you have in your party." The line was thrown. "Blackbeard won't be needing his buried chest anytime soon." The bait was tasty. "It'd be a good score for a young crew looking to make a name for themselves." Hooked.

The Gentleman looked at the others who nodded their heads. Then he looked back to me and did the same. The one with the backwards hands dropped Smee at my feet with a pleasant thud. I took a moment to look down on him and smirk with the satisfaction that can only come from besting a rival.

"This changes nothing," he said through bloodied lips.

"Of course not," I said as I stepped over him to greet my new crewmates.

Chapter Twenty-Eight

The pleasantries didn't last long. As it turned out, Smee was the most experienced sailor of the lot of us. The vote was made seven to two. Only William sided with me and although I applaud myself for sparing Smee's life, I was forced to concede that he should be captain.

"Fine," I told him, "You can be captain. Just get me to Port Royal. I want to be through with this nightmare."

We arrived in Port Royal within days. We pushed the sloop on through the night so that we could beat any dispatch of its theft. She was already loaded with food enough for a crew three times our size. Enough supplies that we could have passed for a charter if questioned.

Smee docked her at the inlet. If we were aboard a larger vessel, our whole story would have to change. Having been raised by sailors, William and I did all the talking. The right phrases and an appropriate fee was all it took. One additional charge and the record showed that we arrived two days earlier. No one on the ship had enough money for a sufficient bribe, so I gave the man the gold coin I found on my father when I buried him. It seemed appropriate that his last gift to me be that I go home in peace.

"William and I are going for clothing," I lied. "We need to fit in." Smee knew better, but there was no nice way to tell a new crew that you were leaving. William's head perked up as if he thought to correct me, but I shot him a look. He had learned enough to know when to be quiet.

"Good idea," Smee responded, obviously taking the hint. They were a dirty looking bunch. Any trained sailor in the King's Navy would spot them for pirates in an instant.

"Just be back by sundown," he said. "We can't risk staying too long." This time, I looked Smee right in the eyes. For a moment, I almost found a glimmer of respect. He could keep it. And if there was a choice between our safe return and my father's watch, Smee could keep that too. We were home. Smee could have the ship, the crew, the watch, and his respect. I had no use for any of it. Not anymore.

"Where to first?" William asked once we were out of earshot.

"I do what I promised to Emily," I smiled, "I'm delivering you to your doorstep."

We walked the paths as if we never left but these same dirty streets and dark taverns were unfamiliar to me now. Nothing was the same as it was years ago. Years ago? It couldn't be.

Then I remembered our time on the island and aboard the *Queen Anne's Revenge.* I looked at William and saw how he'd grown since we left. How much had I changed? Would Emily even recognize us? Worse yet, what if she did and rejected us for who we'd become?

We arrived at the Jukes house before I could piece together

any answers. We stood and stared at the door for way too long before knocking. The knob was lighter than I remembered and not as loud. There was a faint shuffling of feet behind the door. William tensed as if he were ready to run.

"Look sharp," I told him as I forced myself to remain still. The door creaked open and light spilled out onto the street. William and I threw our hands up over our faces to cover our eyes. There was a figure in the door, slight of frame and familiar in shape.

"There are no alms here," the voice said. It was soft but firm. "Now leave here before I call my…"

"We are not looking for charity, my dear lady," I cut in. I lowered my hands and heard a gasp as she saw me. "In fact, I'm here to return something that belongs to you."

It was to no small boost in my pride that she embraced me before William. The fact that she nearly knocked me over into the dirt only enhanced the compliment. I took a moment to hold her before she greeted her brother. With her arms wrapped around my neck, I could fully smell the jasmine in her hair again. She whispered a thank you in my ear before letting go.

I saw her again for the first time as she hugged her brother. She was no longer taller than I was. She also looked far more like a woman than I remembered. Her hair was darker now and reached lower down her back. She turned and looked at me with those piercing eyes.

"I knew you could do it, James," she said through a broad, rare smile. James. I hadn't heard my name said so sweetly in nearly three years. I was reminded of the things William and I did and turned my head away. Would she accept us back into her life so warmly when she hears of our history? I opened my mouth to speak, but William brushed past me. As he moved to enter the house, Emily closed the door behind her.

"What are you doing?" he asked. "We'd like to get cleaned up."

"Not yet," she said, "and not here."

"All's well," I said, a little confused. My courage to confess my sins to Emily faded with each moment and there was still someone I had to see. "I need to get home, too. We can get cleaned up there."

"James," she said. Her tone was serious again. "There is something you need to know."

Chapter Twenty-Nine

Standing over your own grave is an unnerving experience.

It couldn't really be called a grave. There was a tombstone, that was true, but there was no body. There couldn't have been one. I still breathed. My father's grave, right next to mine, was also a lie. They were memorials, at most.

The engravings on my father's headstone told of the man he was: *Daring sailor, Loving husband and father.* Mine were meaningless: *Dutiful and loving child.* Was there no honor in the accomplishments of a child? Was there nothing one could say about wasted potential or unfinished work? Even Pan, who would hardly understand such ideas, was a seeker of adventure and shallow fulfillment. I asked these questions to distract my mind from what I was brought here to see.

My mother's grave was all too real. She lay in the dirt, waiting for us to come back to her. I didn't need to see her body to know she was there. I could feel her. The engravings on her headstone were as meaningless as mine: *Loving wife and mother.*

Accurate as they may have been, they didn't do her justice. There would be no more stories, hugs, or kisses.

This was not how I felt when I found my father, face down on a beach. I could never roll my mother over, bury her, and move on. It was impossible to steel myself. I did little else than sob, tears ran down my cheeks for the first time in years. Emily held me to her chest and I felt at home. Words escaped me, but I had to know, so I tried to speak anyway.

"No," was the best I could do at first, followed by the equally impressive, "When?"

"After she heard about you and your father," Emily said, "she shut herself in the house and wouldn't allow me to let anyone else in." I wished she would stop. She wouldn't. She knew I needed to hear this. "I watched as her health faded. When doctors finally saw her, she was so very weak. She died two months after your funerals. There didn't seem to be any reason for it."

I was taken aback by the comment.

"No reason?" I asked as I began to swell with rage at her lack of emotions. "No reason," I repeated. "I sob now for someone who is taken from me and I find plenty of reason."

"Medically, I mean," she corrected.

For all that Emily was, she was logical. She wouldn't see a cause for prolonged grief. Still, how long did she mourn my death? A month? A week? I knew she'd remember me always, but did she mourn for me at all?

"James, about your father…" she said.

"Captain Ashley," I sneered. I looked back to my father's grave and thought of his body lying in dirt and rocks on some island I'd never be able to find again in a thousand years. "Ashley wasn't where he needed to be and my father died because of his incompetence."

"James, you need to listen," she continued. "Heath brought back news of our fathers' deaths. He had a whole tale to tell about finding the site of the battle and how he fought off Jesse Labette," she added.

"Oh, he found it alright, after arriving a day late," I said. I told her about the meeting in the admiral's office and the battle with Jesse Labette. I told her that Captain Ashley was late and because of that, I watched my father be blown off of the deck of his own ship. I told her about how I found my father and about the dirt mound in which he rots because of the returning hero.

I told her everything except what I was most desperate to say. With every breath I wanted to tell her about Neverland or our time aboard the *Queen Anne's Revenge* or staring into the eyes of Jesse Labette or about the French soldiers, but I couldn't.

Emily was quiet for some time after that. When she finally talked, her words cut through me.

"James," Emily said, "I am engaged to Heath Ashley."

Chapter Thirty

The news of Emily's engagement to Heath Ashley ran over and over in my head until I grew dizzy. My mother lay dead of a broken heart and her husband's betrayer was set to marry the only remaining reason I had for returning to Port Royal. The world spun and I was no longer able to stand. My knees gave out and I crumbled to the ground.

Emily knelt beside me and placed her hand on my shoulder.

"Since our mother died when William and I were young, Father was alone," she said. "We had nannies and maids, but they weren't the same. When Heath returned with news of Father's death, he offered to take care of our estate until I was of the proper age to marry."

"And, of course, you agreed," I snapped. There was more hatred in my voice than I intended. Never before had I disliked her coolness. How could she just forget William and me and agree to marry such a despicable man as Heath Ashley? I tried to stop myself from saying more but I failed.

"How long did you wait after hearing of our deaths before you ran into the arms of your new lover?" The question startled her. My tone was hard, but I had little fight left in me.

"I thought you were dead," she said. "I was afraid I'd have to move back to England. Heath's offer was the only way I'd be able to stay in Port Royal."

"Do you love him?" I asked. I was certain she heard my voice crack as I spoke. I rose from the ground and braced myself for her response. "Well?"

She began to speak but her answer was broken by heavy galloping. The horse and her rider were upon us immediately. The thundering footfalls beat dust into the air so high that the rider was almost unrecognizable. I raised my hands to cover my eyes from the dust. All I saw were shining boots, a red coat, and a ring of keys dangling from the saddle. I looked higher and saw a man with sharp features, a lean build, and dead, grey eyes.

"Emily. What is the meaning of this?" Captain Ashley called out. "Who are these men?" He looked me over with fresh eyes, as though he weren't my father's murderer and my only remaining love's future husband.

"It's James and my brother, Billy," she said. "They've returned to us."

"James…" he started, "…Hoodkins?" He squinted as if I were standing in the thickest fog of London. His angled face twisted to show several recognizable emotions. Disbelief was followed by recognition and shock. He then parted his lips and smiled with everything except his eyes. I didn't know this look when he and I first met, but I knew it now. It was the look of a predator.

"James. William," he finally said with a nod to each of us.

"You look awful. Come back with Emily and me and clean yourselves up before lunch." This wasn't a request as much as it was a command. Captain Ashley had grown quite accustomed to giving orders, it seemed. "We can't have you two looking like a pair of pirates."

Stunned as I was and with nowhere else to go, I followed the predator to his den, knowing full well I might not survive my next meal.

Chapter Thirty-One

The next two hours were a haze. I bathed and clothed myself without thought. The fabric clung and pinched in a way that I'd almost forgotten. When my mind rejoined the present, I was seated at the Jukes's dining room table. Despite my hunger, I ate nothing.

"We'll be wed in one month's time," Captain Ashley said. He looked to Emily, who was seated next to him. He held her hand too tightly to be comfortable. The few times she broke free, he grasped it and rested it back on the table.

"By then, you'll make admiral for sure," I said. The statement gave him pause, but only for a moment. His eyes narrowed. A grin stretched across his face.

"I'm many years away from that," he said. "To make admiral, I'd have to put in as many years as your father did. Even then, the promotion to admiral is not a guarantee."

"Of course not," I said. "You'd have to be some kind of hero." William dropped his fork. Emily froze mid-bite. Captain

Ashley just smirked.

"You're angry at me for the way I greeted you earlier," Captain Ashley said. "You'll have to excuse my abruptness. It's been an exciting day. I just arrested a small group of pirates who docked a sloop this morning."

"No," William gasped. I shot him a look that quieted him for the rest of the meal. He hadn't said much so far and I wanted to keep it that way. I didn't know if Captain Ashley caught on to William's comment, but Emily certainly did. She visibly stiffened.

"Indeed," Captain Ashley responded. "I have no doubt that there are more of them. They refuse to talk, but I'm sure our interrogators will get something out of them before they're hanged tomorrow morning." His eyes never left mine. He was searching for something. Guilt? Remorse? As it was, William's fidgeting gave our guilt away faster than a full confession. Why was Heath Ashley so interested in my reaction?

"They put up quite a fight," he added. "I had to rap one over the head with the hilt of my sword." I was curious to ask which, but couldn't without giving myself up. Although none of them were my favorite person, there wasn't one I'd favor less than Captain Ashley.

"A sloop is a small vessel," I said. "However did you know to look for her crew over any other ship?"

"Interestingly enough, the information came to me," Captain Ashley said. "An innkeeper gave me this." He tossed the gold coin down on the table in front of me. I stifled the appearance of recognizing it, but it was undoubtedly my father's coin. I could tell by the markings. "He told me that the dockworker paid his tab with it. Once I spoke to the dock worker, I had all the information I needed to make the arrest."

If he spoke to the dock worker, then surely he was given a

description of the two men who negotiated the price. He'd know how many men were on the ship and how we were eager to change our time of arrival. Still, there was something that was bothering me.

"What's so important about that coin?" I asked, genuinely curious. "It could be from anywhere."

"No, it can't," he said. "It's your father's. Besides, one of the pirates had this." He reached into his jacket pocket and pulled a familiar gold watch. My father's watch. The watch that Smee took from me the day he brought William and me aboard the *Queen Anne's Revenge.* "The coin and the watch are your father's, which means that these pirates were a part of Jesse Labette's crew at the time of his death and can lead me to him."

Whatever the story was behind the coin, there was no denying the connection I had to that watch. If he was telling the truth, no one else would have had possession of either item aside from my father. Even the possibility that any pirate on Labette's ship had stolen them seemed unlikely while two pirates were missing and William and I were seated in front of him.

Then my mind snapped to attention. This was his game. He didn't want to tell Emily of our deeds. He knew that would never work. He wanted us to admit it to her ourselves so that we would be forever ruined in her eyes.

"Which reminds me," Captain Ashley said. "You never did tell us of your harrowing rescue and return to Port Royal." The trap was sprung and we were caught in his net. Emily's eyes shot back and forth between William and me. I could tell by her stares that she'd figured us out. It was over. I opened my mouth to talk, but she interrupted me.

"Excuse me," she said. "There's work around the house that must be done." Her voice was nearly as shaky as her attempt to stand.

"Of course, my dear," Captain Ashley said. He released her hand and we all rose as the lady left. She did not look back at us as she went. Once she was gone, I gave in to my curiosity.

"How would you know that the coin is my father's?" I asked.

"It's from a rare chest of native treasures that only three men know about." He pulled his shirt open to reveal an identical gold coin dangling from a silver chain. "We each keep one as a reminder. Terms of our fortune, you can say."

"What do you mean?" I asked.

"It's unclaimed treasure, so we claimed it. Swearing to secrecy, of course," he smiled wickedly. "Every so often, we take a little to further our careers or our properties."

"Piracy?" William stammered.

"Opportunity," Ashley corrected and turned to me. "Your father and I ambushed and sank a small armada of pirate ships not too far south and west of here," he told me. "Some of the savages swam ashore and we took boats to follow."

"My captain and I found it first. Jonathan stumbled upon us already dividing up our stakes. He insisted that we bring it back to the ship and pay our share to the crown. Always procedures with him. Still, my captain is a very convincing man and, in the end, your father wasn't as noble as he let on."

"That's not true," I growled. My fists clenched at the thought of what he was suggesting.

"Oh, it most certainly is," he sneered at me. "In fact, since that day, every pirate ship we took, we added to the pile of our fortune."

"And now you have a much larger cut of that pile," I snarled at him. "My father's death has played out well for you, hasn't it?" He looked at me with a newly heavy seriousness.

"I never wanted your father dead," he told me. "I just wanted him to admit to himself the man he was."

"Wait," William said. "My father knew about this?"

"Harrison knew nothing, which was his role in life," Heath said. "A big, dumb, reliable ox for Jonathan to order around. If Jonathan actually respected him, I'm sure he would have told him."

"I won't let you slander my father's name," I told him.

"Neither of you are in any position to clear it," Captain Ashley stepped over to the fireplace and shuffled through some papers. "I hope you understand the gravity of your actions," he said over his shoulder before placing a note on the table. I picked it up and read it in disbelief.

Emily,

I have found William and James, or rather, they have found me. They are alive but there is something you need to know.

They were on the ships raiding Charles Town. James is using the name Hook and looks every bit the pirate. I barely recognized him or William. They're both so hardened and cold.

James told me that they are trying to get back to Port Royal, but I don't see how anyone can return from such a life.

I'm sorry. I wish I had better news.

Regrettably,
Thomas Darling

"As caretaker of the Jukes' estate," Captain Ashley said. "I receive all mail sent to this residence. I spared Emily from reading it. Sadly, I didn't get to your poor mother in time." My heart sank. I looked up at the man who had beaten me.

"So," he said, "does the dread pirate, Hook, prefer his hanging in the morning or in the evening?"

Before I had a chance to respond, William leapt onto the table and dove at Captain Ashley. They tumbled to the floor and I was left dumbfounded. I quickly came to the conclusion that when all civilized action was exhausted, the savagery that lies within all of us was the only answer. I folded the letter into my pocket and joined the tumble.

Our advantage was short lived. William was strong and we were two to his one, but Captain Ashley was a trained killer. We both wound up lying on the floor, backs to the fire, with an enraged Captain Ashley standing over us. He pulled out his pistol and took a steady aim.

"There will be no noose for you," he said, "no crowd to view your deaths. You will die alone and uncelebrated, like every pirate should."

I stared him down boldly, knowing that this was the end. I had traveled this far only to be shot by the man who abandoned my father to his death. I knew that similar thoughts were going through William's mind as well.

As I awaited the click of the hammer and the burst of gunfire, I heard the unexpected crash of glass. Heath Ashley slumped to the floor and my Emily rushed to us.

"Hurry," she said, "there are more on the way." In our shock, she grabbed us both by the wrist and led us to the window. We saw five men breaking down the front door. I grabbed my father's coin and watch before we opened the window and climbed down the grate to the side.

"Why?" I asked once we reached the ground. I tried to come up with more to say but failed.

"When your mother died," she said, "I thought I lost the last part of you. I'm not losing either of you again."

"What about Captain Ashley?" I asked her.

"He's after the estate," she said. "If he wants it, he can have it." She mounted one of the horses left by the soldiers. "So, what are you waiting for? Let's go get your ship back."

"Not yet," I told her. William and I mounted horses of our own. "If we're sailing, we'll need my crew."

"Fine," Emily said. She sidled over to Heath Ashley's horse and threw me the ring of keys on his saddle. "You'll need these."

"We'll meet up at dusk," I said. "You know where."

Chapter Thirty-Two

My mind chased ideas that came and went as fast as our horses rode into town. I didn't need to think about how to get to the holding cells. I'd seen them a dozen times in my youth. My mind was occupied with how William and I were going to overcome British soldiers.

We approached the jailhouse without one shred of a plan. We couldn't run in shooting, we'd surely end up dead. Nor did we have the time for anything fancy. However, I did remember something that could help. William and I dismounted and crept around the back of the building. I remembered a small grating in the alley where one could look in and see the prisoners.

Captain Ashley was telling the truth. The entire crew was in this cell. Starkey, the gentleman, and Cecco, the Italian, sat in one cell. Noodler, with the backwards hands, was in the second with the others. I didn't see Smee right away, but found him lying in the cot behind Cecco.

There were two guards in the lower area. One seated. One

standing. There were always two at the desk, plus the interrogator, made five. I felt the edge of paper in my pocket and the seed of a plan formed in my mind. I waited for one of them to look over. Cecco saw me first and elbowed Starkey quietly. He motioned to Noodler, then slid over to catch the keys as I dropped them through the grate. I pointed to the two guards and then back at Starkey, letting him know that they were his responsibility. I turned to William and told him, "Follow my lead."

Dressed as we were, we looked respectable. That should get us through the door. I pounded my fist against the heavy door. Metal scraped against the wood and a man peered through a slat.

"What is it?" he asked.

"I have a message from Captain Ashley," I told him. William shot me a surprised look but I continued, "He has captured the two missing pirates at the Jukes's household and requires the presence of the interrogator." The bolt slid and the door opened with a creak.

William and I stepped through and were greeted by three men. Two were husky soldiers. The other was a sharper, leaner man, who had to be interrogator. I pulled Thomas Darling's letter from my pocket and waved it in the air.

"This correspondence demands your presence at the Jukes' household with your instruments immediately," I told him. Captain Ashley must have garnered an impressive reputation at my father's expense because the interrogator nearly jumped out of his skin as he bolted through the door. One of the husky soldiers followed him out, leaving only one soldier behind the desk.

"Hand it here," he said. I must have looked at him blankly because he said it again, this time more forcefully. "The letter. Hand it over." I gave it to him. I watched as his face twisted with confusion. "What is the meaning of this?"

As the echo of gunfire sounded from the cells, the soldier turned and William and I lunged at him. William held him as I wrestled his pistol away and fired. The bullet hit him high in the chest and dropped him to the floor.

William and I rushed to the cell. We found one soldier already dead at the feet of Cecco, who now held the soldier's pistol. The other soldier was being held against the bars by Noodler and the others, while Skarkey attempted to unlock their cell door.

There was no time to waste. Someone must have heard the gunfire. On the table next to me were the items that were confiscated during the arrest. Of the selection of knives and tools was a single boarding hook. I grabbed it and swung a hard overhand strike to the soldier being held against the bars. The hook sank deep in the soldier's chest. I must have hit the heart, because blood gushed out onto the floor. It wasn't clean, but it ended quickly.

"Round up the men," I shouted. "It's time to leave." The satisfaction of giving orders was only dulled by the feeling that something was wrong. Something was missing. It took me a moment to figure out what it was.

"Where's Smee?" I asked. It wasn't that I didn't notice his presence. What I noticed most was the absence of his objection to me being the one to give orders. Noodler pointed a backwards finger at the far cell.

Smee was now sitting upright on his cot. As I walked towards him, I saw that his head was wrapped with cloth and there was dried blood down the side of his face, staining the hair that was starting to grey slightly at the sides. And then I remembered what Captain Ashley said about having to strike one of the pirates with the hilt of his sword. Somehow, I never expected it to be Smee.

"How bad are you hurt?" I asked. Smee turned to me slowly

and smiled. This smile was not that of a predator. There was no hidden intent. This was a true smile and considering the man supplying it, it was far more terrifying.

"What are my orders, Captain?" he asked. Confused, I looked to Starkey for an answer. He just shook his head. Cecco, Noodler and the others did the same.

"We have to go now, Smee," I told him. Obediently, he nodded and stood. He stumbled and I caught him. I surprised even myself that I didn't let him fall. After all the beatings he gave me, Smee didn't deserve my sympathy. But then I'd never seen him so weak and defeated.

"It's me," he stuttered quietly.

"Yes," I told him. "Your name is Smee."

"No, IT'S ME!" he yelled. "What I was saying when they found me." He turned his glassy eyes up to meet mine. "It's me." I looked at him for a moment before remembering Jesse Labette's story of how Smee came aboard the *Queen Anne's Revenge*.

"I was on a freighter with my parents. We were attacked by pirates," Smee began. "There were so many. They killed my father and the captain." His breath was shallow between statements. "I managed to throttle one to death. I grabbed for my mother to take her below deck. She turned and ran me through the gut." He wrenched over and held his stomach as though the wound were still fresh. "I heard her cries as I tumbled overboard. 'It's me,' I kept saying. 'It's me.'"

Until now, the idea of leaving him behind had been very real. Now, I couldn't seem to bring myself to let him fall. So much of his life was taken by pirates and even more was taken by Heath Ashley. If there was such a thing as justice, abandoning Smee would not serve its purposes.

"Do you remember your name?" I asked him.

"What good is it?" he said. "I'm Smee just like you're Hook." He looked at me with glassy eyes and began to blubber. I covered his face and shook him.

"Look sharp," I barked.

"Is the ship where we left it?" I asked. Smee regained his composure before he answered.

"Y—Yes, but there are soldiers on her now." I looked down at the bodies of the three soldiers at our feet.

"I'm sure I'll think of something," I told him. Then, shakily, Smee put one foot in front of the other and followed me out of the cell.

Chapter Thirty-Three

Recovering the ship was easier than expected. William set fire to the jail cell, drawing most of the soldiers and local officials away from the pier. The two adjacent buildings went up in minutes. By the time we reached the sloop, that whole block was engulfed in black smoke. We killed the two soldiers aboard the ship quickly. We took our time with the dock keeper.

We took the sloop around the island to the spot where I was to meet Emily. You know where, I told her. Though small, the ship was still too large to take safely into the lagoon. We dropped anchor off-shore and I prepared a boat.

"Wait here," I told them. "I'll be bringing back another."

"What makes you think we won't leave you?" Cecco said with a smirk. William and Smee visibly tensed, but one look from me settled them. I pulled a boarding hook out of my coat pocket and held it up to my eye.

"By now I'm sure you've learned better," I joked. No one laughed. "There are treasures to be found and more cities to burn," I told them. "Besides, I'll be but a moment."

With that, I began rowing to the shore. I left William behind. He didn't need to be a part of this. This was between me and Emily.

Thinking of her brought back all the same worries over whether she could truly accept me. Yes, she chose me over Captain Ashley back at the house. That should be enough, but I needed to know. Questions ran through my mind with each stroke of the oar against the water. Did she save me because she knew Captain Ashley was about to kill me or because she knew me and wanted me just the same?

I reached the shore and looked up at the growth hanging over the rocky wall. The climb up the steep side of the cliff was hard, but I remembered the way. Of all the changes I had seen, this was the one place that remained the same.

More thoughts burned in my mind with each step. What if she did accept me wholly and completely? The life I had dreamt of returning to was long dead. As I reached the top of the rocky overhang, with blood pounding in my ears, I realized that all the days of my future depended on the next few minutes.

"Emily?" I called out. For a moment, I wondered if she was even coming. When I found her, she was sitting on the rocks we used to lay on as children. Her golden hair and slender frame were outlined by the reflection of the setting sun in the lagoon. Infinite moments of perfection.

"I've been here for a few minutes now," she said. She smiled over her shoulder at me and ran into my arms. She broke from me only to reach back behind the rocks. "I think this belongs to you," she said as she handed me a treasure beyond words. I grasped my father's sword, noting how much lighter it was in my hands now than the last time I held it.

"How did you get this?" I asked her. "It was on the ship when it sank."

"Captain Ashley brought it back as part of the proof of our fathers' deaths. By rights, it belongs to you."

I thanked her and clutched the last remaining piece of my father. Tied to the hilt, was my mother's old cloth.

"It is something to remember them both," she said. "Almost like being with them again." One tear ran down my cheek. Memories returned to me as I thought that the last time I saw this sword I was with... Pan. I then remembered everything that happened afterwards.

"There's so much I still need to tell you," I said.

"Do you?" she asked. There was a familiar coolness in her voice. She was preparing herself for another story like Peter Pan. I opened my mouth to speak, but she placed a hand on my cheek and added, "I knew you would do whatever it took to keep your promise to me." Her eyes begged me not to say anymore. Every person has a threshold of understanding. Perhaps she knew hers better than most.

There was a breath behind some bushes and a pause that lasted a second too long. The click of a pistol was deafening in the silent woods. The brilliant scarlet coat told me who it was before he spoke.

"Do you think I don't know my own bride to be?" Captain Ashley smirked. He stepped out from where he'd been hiding and pointed the pistol at me. "She'd come here often and just stare off. I thought it had to do with her father or brother or something. If I'd known it was over you, I'd have put an end to it." Up until this point, I had given up all hope that Emily had mourned me for long. She didn't seem the type. My joy at finding out otherwise was somewhat diminished by threat of death, but not by much.

"At least," Captain Ashley said, "I can finally put an end

to you." He fired without the hint of doubt or hesitation. The shot thundered in the air, but the bullet never reached me. Before I could react, Emily was in my arms. I felt the bullet hit her back. She looked at me in disbelief as her body went heavy and tumbled to the ground.

Chapter Thirty-Four

I cradled Emily as each cough brought blood to her lips and jerked her body to the side. Her eyes, once so full of life, fell slowly into death. I didn't cry. I was strong for her.

"James," she gasped. "I tried to ... tell you before..." She began to go limp and I felt her grasp weaken on my shoulder.

"No!" I yelled. "Stay with me." She lifted her head and summoned her strength to speak one final time.

"Ashley... It's not his fault," she coughed. More blood came.

"Impossible," I told her. Heath Ashley had aimed and fired. He intended to kill me and she got in the way. There was no one else to blame for the fault. I looked to her to explain, but I was too late. I watched the light in her eyes fade.

For an untold time, I forgot Captain Ashley was even there. I was only reminded when I heard him whisper, "Oh, my god, what have I done?" I turned to see my lover's killer. Ashley lowered his pistol in shock. The color drained from his features to match his dull, grey eyes. Between breaths, he exhaled "Oh Lord, please forgive me."

"You don't get to mourn her," I snarled at him. My words didn't budge him an inch. He stood, mouth agape, over Emily's body. The body of the last pure thing I had in this world.

My body took over where my mind would have cautioned. I pulled my father's sword from its sheath and struck at Captain Ashley. He came to his senses enough to parry the blow with the pistol in his hand. He dodged the next three swipes as well.

He struck me with the butt of his pistol and got distance. By the time I turned, I saw that he shed his vivid red coat and drew his own sword into guard. There was no talking. There were no taunts. This was a fight to the death without quarter given or received. If I was to die, let it be by Emily's side as it should have been a lifetime from now. No day beyond this moment was worth it if he still breathed.

Heath Ashley stood upright, holding his sword low at his hip, but at an upward angle. I circled him to his left and drew the boarding hook out from within my coat. I struck twice high and thrust low. He blocked each strike before shoving me back and pushing his attack. He feinted right and unleashed a rapid combination of thrusts and strikes that the expression on his face suggested would certainly end me.

I parried and cut him, just barely, with a low, upward rip across his chest using the hook. His expression changed from one of certainty, to shock, then settled on embarrassment mixed with disgust.

"You dirty, sickly, little savage!" he cried out. He drew his breath to say more, but I pressed the attack. Reflexively, he parried and slashed me across my back. I barely felt the sting. He kicked me down and prepared the killing blow.

Then the most unusual event occurred. His foot caught a hidden rock in the tall grass and his sword drove deep into the grass next to me. I recovered quickly enough to jab him in the ribs with the point of my sword.

Enraged, he swiped and missed, his back foot caught in a shallow patch of mud. I thrust high and caught him in the shoulder.

It is then that I realized that I did not stop to recognize my advantage. Captain Ashley may have been the more accomplished swordsman, but this was my terrain. Here, I knew everything. Every rock, every soft patch of grass, every spot where your foot sank just a little bit deeper than you expected. Especially in the fading light of dusk, here I was unbeatable.

He began to retreat and found himself with his back against the cliff's edge. He looked down, then back to me with certainty that only one of us would survive the next exchange.

Captain Ashley swiped high. His sword caught my hook and sent it spinning into the bushes. He charged and thrust downward, but I feinted left, measured the distance, and stepped hard with my lead foot, driving the point of my sword through his midsection. I pushed it straight to the hilt and looked him dead in the face so that I could savor every subtle twitch.

He dropped his sword in the grass as blood oozed down his arm. His face was a mixture of sadness and loss, like one who had grand dreams taken from him.

His death wasn't just for me. It was for the others. For Emily. For my mother. For William. For my father and Mr. Jukes. Yes, even for Smee. For them and many more I drew my sword out of him and kicked him over the side and down into the lagoon.

An icy cool ran through me as I knelt next to Emily's forever still body and covered her with my coat. I said my final words, knowing she would have a grave, a tombstone, and a proper burial here in Port Royal. I left everything that James Hoodkins was with her, not just to rest, but so that she might know at least part of the way to heaven.

I rose to my feet, grabbed Heath Ashley's bold red jacket, and headed down the cliff solely as Captain Hook.

When I returned to the ship and gave the order to make sail, only William hesitated. As his captain, I owed him no explanation. As his friend, I owed him some form of the truth.

"She's staying," I told him. He looked at my new coat and the blood on my hands but said nothing. I glanced down at my stained clothes and added, "I gave her my coat. It was cleaner than Captain Ashley's." He nodded and asked no further questions. Our time on the island those years ago taught him the value of holding fast to a fantasy.

"Course and heading, Captain?" Starkey asked. Black smoke billowed in the distance from the blaze we set earlier. Firelight danced on dark clouds as a necessary plan formed in my mind.

"Southeast," I told him. He joined the others in seamless harmony. They tethered and hitched, all with an unspoken understanding of their roles. They were silent, focused, and efficient, nearly ready for what was coming next.

"Mr. Starkey," I called out across the deck of the sloop. He turned his head, never breaking the rhythm of the work. "Have you ever heard of the *Jolly Roger*?"

Chapter Thirty-Five

Two years of gathering information through trade and raid brought us to the morning we retook my father's ship. William and I stood shoulder to shoulder and watched the sunrise bathe the *Jolly Roger* in rich orange and yellow rays. Our eyes tracked the growing dark spot that crested the horizon and crept across the water towards us.

The lessons I learned as a boy clung to me tightly. More so than when we killed the male croc on the island, the plan to lead Jesse Labette to his death was carefully thought out.

Labette had been looking for a new partner in trade since the news of Blackbeard's death last November at Ocracoke Island. It seemed that Blackbeard let himself get ambushed by British ships and a few hired sloops. His guns managed to blow one sloop aside, but the drinking he and his men did the night before dulled their wits to the point of folly. The heroic and infinitely civilized first lieutenant who organized the attack hung Blackbeard's head on the Bowsprit of his ship as a trophy.

We were one night's sail away of where the raid of Charles Town took place when we heard. Each man took the news in his own way. Some men sang songs of their fallen hero. Others, William included, fell silent for hours. Smee sobbed quietly for the loss of a second father. I understood how he felt but spoke to no one about it.

Blackbeard had been my guide through this second life. In many ways, he shaped me as much as my true father and as repayment I ran his ship aground. Looking back, I didn't regret betraying him. It seemed fitting somehow.

Out of respect for the man who taught me so much, I gave Blackbeard an hour's reflection before setting my mind to the task at hand. Unlike the death of my true father, I was now a man and a man doesn't waste such a fine opportunity.

After a quick robbery of a French port, we had enough louis-d'ors to entice Jesse Labette to meet me here.

"You're joining me in the cabin," I said to William. "John Silver's the new Quartermaster. He'll be in the cabin, alongside Labette." William grunted his understanding and clenched his fists with anticipation. He and Silver nearly had it out last time and he was as eager as I was to draw blood today. "I want him alive," I told him. William stopped mid-breath and turned to me with a puzzled look. Realizing that I was being greedy, I allowed him a concession, "Bruised, but unhurt." A broad grin of genuine happiness stretched across his face.

The *Jolly Roger*, or the *Britannia* as she was named under my father's command, was a tall, older brigantine. She approached and made her true size clear by the shadow she cast on our sloop. We would be fools to attack her directly. Labette would not need to trouble himself with any of the dozens of guns on the ship. One shot from Long Tom would end us for certain.

"Ahoy," called a ragged man aboard the *Jolly Roger*. I returned the greeting and nodded to Cecco and Starkey, who began setting the plan into motion. William, Smee, and I stood along the railing while the men on deck tethered lines to hooks and cast them onto the *Jolly Roger*. They drew the ships closer to one another and extended planks across each deck. The crew of the brigantine greeted us with fake smiles and forced cheers. Throughout this, I remained steady, watching each man's movement.

A cold chill ran through me as we stepped onto the plank that connected the two ships. The *Jolly Roger* groaned and growled, but I steeled myself to her threats. Her crew watched us out of the sides of their eyes, nearly twice our number and armed to the teeth.

Then I saw him. Jesse Labette, the murderer of my father, whose tall slender frame was capped by the same wide-brimmed black hat, grinned at me with a sparkle of recognition in his eyes. To his left was John Silver, taller and broader than I remembered him. To his right was the same ragged sailor that hailed our ship earlier.

William, Smee, and I lined ourselves up, facing our prey. Labette stepped forward and bowed.

"Welcome aboard the *Jolly Roger*, Captain Hook," he said. "I hear you have French treasures for trade."

"That, and much more, Captain Labette," I told him. He approached me with his arms outstretched and laughed broadly.

"Come, Captain Hook," he cackled. "You can teach me what more there is to life than French women and French money." He led us to the door of the captain's quarters. Smee and the ragged pirate waited outside while Labette and Silver walked into the cabin. William ducked through the doorway and looked back as if to ask if I was coming. I nodded and stepped inside.

The room was as I remembered it from my youth. Wall for

wall. Angle for angle. Jesse Labette sat behind an oak desk and removed his hat, revealing long hair that was tightly pulled back. Its fair color framed his stern, lean face. When the door shut behind me, I breathed a small sigh of relief, knowing that my part of the plan was over. Now that we were alone, I sat opposite Labette and smiled with everything except for my eyes.

"So, Captain Hook," Jesse Labette said. "Tell me about my louis-d'ors."

"They're not yours yet," I told him. "And you'll have however much you can get in even trade."

"How much could you have on such a small ship?" he asked. He and John Silver shared a look. No doubt they planned to take the money regardless of what was agreed to here. It was fortunate for me that my plan was already in motion.

"Enough to bring you to me," I said.

"Don't waste my time," he snarled. "I'm due south of Bermuda in two days."

"You'll be late," William said not quietly enough to be ignored. Jesse Labette and John Silver snapped a look to William and then to each other, unsure of what to make of the comment.

"Forgive Bill Jukes," I said. "He's something of a wonder in predicting storms." A few uneasy moments passed before Labette leaned forward to speak again.

"And what is it that you have to trade other than money?" he asked.

"Information," I told him. He leaned back and snorted his mistrust. Information was always a gamble in the world of trade. I decided to tempt him further, "It is a matter of life and death."

"Is it now?" he said, leaning in again. "Whose?"

"Yours," William said. I shot him a look that silenced him

for the rest of the negotiation. Labette's face visibly reddened as he narrowed his piercing gaze at William.

"Your mate wouldn't be threatening me, would he?"

"Certainly not," I told him. "I happen to know that two men aboard your ship have done little but plan your death for years." He looked from William to me without changing his sour expression. He breathed deeply twice before letting loose with a full-bellied laugh.

"My death?" he bellowed. "And what have I done to earn such ire?" he added with mock innocence. John Silver joined in with laughter of his own.

"You killed their fathers when you took this ship," I told him through gritted teeth.

"That's all?" he cackled. "I had to take this brig. Two shots from this old girl and I had to scrap my last ship. She was in a bad way, but we fixed her up fine."

"Their lives mean nothing?" I asked him.

"I've killed scores of fathers and I've sunk a dozen ships." He and Silver continued their hearty laughter so loudly that they failed to hear a loud thud below deck. "But if the two men you speak of were from this ship, they must be ghosts or shades. All hands were lost."

"Not all hands," I told him. "And although they may be shades of themselves, they are here." This time, we all heard the tumbling and shouting beneath us. Labette looked to Silver, then back to me. Visibly concerned, he stopped laughing and straightened himself.

"Alright," he said, "Who?"

"No," I told him. "Not until we name a price." The first gunshots thundered in our ears as the rumble spilled out from below onto the main deck.

"Grain?" he offered. "Dried fruit or meat?"

"No," I told him. Grunts, just outside of the door, rose to a gurgled scream and ended in silence. Flashes of panic began to crack Jesse Labette's unshakable façade. "Not enough."

"Not enough?" he cried. "Fine, silver? ... gold?" He looked to us before throwing his hands up in anger. "What more is there?"

The speed at which I drew my hook from within my coat and plunged it into his chest did nothing to take away the enjoyment of the job. It was a high, hard, overhand strike that purposely just missed his heart. I wondered if he thought, even for the briefest moment, that the light that so blinded his eyes was from heaven. He had to know that men like us didn't see heaven. At best, we may only get halfway there.

"Blood," I told him.

William was on John Silver before the first gurgles of spittle came forth from Labette's mouth. The noise from their brawl nearly eclipsed the roar from outside the cabin. It was a sound not unlike that of pounding beef with a wide mallet mixed with muffled cries, but I didn't turn to look. My eyes were fixed on Labette's increasingly distant gaze.

"Get us outside," I told William. With the order given, William hoisted John Silver over his shoulder and heaved the broad man through the door, splintering it to pieces.

"Where do you think you're going?" William snickered as he ducked through the doorway and lumbered after him.

Using the hook, I dragged Labette out of the cabin and into the chaos on the deck of the ship. When I got to the main mast, I pulled my still sparkling hook from his chest and propped him up in time to watch his crew fall at my hands.

He saw it all. Smee thrust his sword into one pirate after another, joyously calling out "Johnny Corkscrew" as he twisted the blade. Starkey stabbed not one, but two men at the same time before gunning down a third. Noodler strangled the pirate with the salt-crusted beard using only his backwards hands. Cecco, the Italian, wrapped his chains around a neck of one man and stabbed at another. Robert Mullins, Alf Mason, Skylights, Ed Teynte, and a dozen more ravaged their way through the ship.

Out of something similar to professional courtesy, I called to Smee. The stout Irishman pried a blunderbuss out from a dead man's hands and blasted Labette's chest open before kicking him over the bow. We stood at the railing for several seconds and watched the dread pirate bob and float before finally sinking into the cold waters below.

As I turned to rejoin the fray, one pirate lunged after me with a sword. William stopped him as one would stop a child. He crushed the pirate's hands around the hilt, disarmed him, and killed him before returning to continue throttling John Silver.

"Enough!" I barked. Each of my men pulled back to a ready position. The remaining men in Labette's crew recovered their footing and stared at each other in confusion, wondering why they were still breathing. "My fight isn't with you. We're done here," I told them, then looked to John Silver, who was holding his side. "Nearly."

A sword stuck out from the back of a man at my feet. I pulled it and threw it down in front of John Silver.

"Pick it up," I told him. He went for it at first, but stopped to look at William, who just smiled. He turned to grab for it a second time, but stopped again when he met my eyes, my drawn sword, and my ready guard. He stopped for a breath of time and considered himself carefully, perhaps for the first time.

"If we fight, you'd kill me," he said.

"Without hesitation," I told him. He looked to William, then back down at the sword again before meeting my eyes.

"So why don't you?" he asked.

"Because, I owe you," I said, lowering my sword. "In spite of yourself, you taught me a valuable lesson." I raised my father's sword, measured the distance, stepped hard with my lead foot, and drove the point of it just short of the tip of his nose. "This thrust ended the life of my father's betrayer and my lover's killer." He stared at it but dared not swat it away. "And in return for your lesson, I offer this one in return." I drew the sword back and waved it around at the carnage I had created.

"How'd you do this?" he asked. "We had you out-manned and out-gunned."

"Patience," I told him. "Nothing a little planning couldn't take care of. Years ago, I noticed that Jesse Labette ran this ship with a skeleton crew. Either he relied too heavily on Long Tom or he preferred to split any prizes in as few ways as possible." Silver bowed his head and looked up again, silently admitting that I guessed correctly on both tries. "Our haul of louis-d'ors drew him in. Once the ships were tethered, I had my crew take to the water and swim unseen to the far side of the *Jolly Roger*. There, they were able to scale the far side and get in through the cannon hatches." Silver and his remaining crewmates shot looks of accusation at one another.

"It wasn't your fault," I said. "Your crew was on the near side of the ship in preparation for a more traditional double-cross. I'm sorry to disappoint you." William and Starkey stifled a laugh between themselves. Smee, Noodler, and Cecco cackled and hooted loudly.

"Now, leave my ship and tell every man you see who it was that let you live. Tell them that Captain Hook now commands the *Jolly Roger*."

Silver stared at the sword at his feet for several seconds before turning to the boards that bridge the two ships. William and the rest of my crew hustled the men onto the sloop and tied them to the masts. We loaded the cannons and nearly all of the supplies onto the *Jolly Roger* before separating the ships. When we were at a distance, Cecco threw a knife that stuck into the mast beside John Silver's head.

"He'll come after you," William told me as we watched Silver and his men cut their restraints.

"I think not," I told him. "He's smart enough to learn, but not smart enough to be a threat to us." William looked almost disappointed, so I added, "But, since we tried it my way, if he does come, he's yours to deal with."

So set the first sun on my days as captain of my father's ship. With both his betrayer, Heath Ashley, and his killer, Jesse Labette, dead at my hands, the avenging of my father's death was complete. Only the redemption of his name remained.

Dusk

Chapter Thirty-Six

The *Triumph*, and her prize, the *Jolly Roger*, sail away from the storm at last. The roar of the water and the clash of now distant thunder make all noise outside of the brig impossible to hear.

Deep within the hull of the *Triumph*, Admiral Charles Price chronicles the deeds of the nefarious Captain Hook before the pirate's trial and execution at Port Royal. He drafts between cups of tea, brought to him by the two guards who watch the pirate. He thanks the shorter guard, the one whose hair slightly grays at the sides, for bringing him a fresh cup.

"This is a fantastic story," Admiral Price comments as he scratches his parchment. He pauses to look up at the pirate. "You have names and dates, yes, but not the slightest shred of proof."

"I have the *Jolly Roger*…" Hook says.

"Had the *Jolly Roger*," Admiral Price corrects. "That ship is now the possession of the Royal Navy."

"Still," Hook smirks, "it proves that I killed Labette."

"Perhaps." He picks up the cup of tea, but pauses before drinking it. "Tell me, what happens when one beast swallows another? Does he grow stronger for the victory or is he less of what he was from the fight?"

"Both," Hook answers.

"And why keep the name, *Jolly Roger*?" Price asks before placing the cup back on the saucer and picking up his quill again. "If it was the *Britannia*, why not name it as such?"

"She'll be the *Jolly Roger* as long as I must do Evil in Good's name," Hook tells him. "The name was needed to draw in the last of those who wronged my father."

"You crossed off the two on your list," Admiral Price says. "Captain Ashley and Jesse Labette."

"The Betrayer and the Murderer," Hook says. "A third still breathes."

"Yes," Admiral Price says, checking his pages, "you mentioned a third."

"Only the Corruptor remains," Captain Hook says coldly.

"These are still naught but stories," Admiral Price says, folding the parchments.

"If proof is what you need," Captain Hook reaches into his pocket and draws out two gold coins. He throws them onto the admiral's desk. "These coins, the ones my father and Captain Ashley wore around their necks, are the ones you gave them to bind them into theft and piracy." Admiral Price picks them up and examines them closely. "You should recognize them, Admiral. They are identical to the one you wear as well."

Admiral Price draws his chair back from the desk. He puts a hand on his chest in reflex then takes it away.

"Were you not at one time the captain of Heath Ashley?" Hook asks. "You claimed native treasures in secret and bound an honest man to dishonesty. Youthful rage blinded me to Captain Ashley's words, but years at sea have brought me patient clarity."

"Impossible," Admiral Price says, truly looking at James Hook for the first time.

"You were in that meeting to arrange the capture of Jesse Labette," James continues. "No doubt, you conspired to betray my father to his death, being that you two stood the most to gain."

Admiral Price reaches his hand into his shirt and pulls out a gold coin on a silver chain. "This is not proof enough of your story, but it is enough to damage the reputations of fine sailors."

"Yes," Hook admits, "scandal enough to shake the King's Navy to its knees." Admiral Price sits staring at the coins in front of him for a moment. Then he takes them and shoves them into his coat pocket.

"The solution, it seems," Admiral Price chuckles, "is to be sure that you never get the chance to talk." He looks at the two guards who return a stifled laugh. Satisfied with all he had written, Admiral Price stacks his parchment and lays down his quill. "We'll hang you on the ship and present your corpse upon our return."

"You would put me on display, would you?" Captain Hook asks. "How unfittingly barbaric behavior for a gentleman of your standing. Poor form, indeed."

"It is common practice for pirates," Admiral Price says. "All will be remedied when you are dead."

Admiral Price reaches for his cup and sips some tea.

"My thoughts exactly," Hook says as he parts his lips into a smile.

It begins with a cough. Admiral Price brings his hands to his chest as if a cannon had just blasted a hole through it.

The larger crewman starts his quartet in low tones at first.

"To have so much and lose it all,
Is such a fearful trip.
You'll gag. You'll choke. God snuffs your flame.
It ends with just one sip."

The admiral's face first turns red like the setting sun then blue
like the sky at noon. He clasps his throat and tumbles to the floor.

"Even diluted in tea, the poison works quickly," Hook says.
"Don't you agree, Admiral?" Admiral Price can no longer speak
words, but looks at Captain Hook with questioning eyes. "The
uniforms," Hook says. Admiral Price's eyes flash with understanding
and horror. Hook leans down to him and confirms his terror. "The
men aboard the *Jolly Roger* weren't British sailors."

Captain Hook looks to the guard whose hair slightly grays at
the sides and says, "I assume all went according to plan?"

"Indeed, sir," Smee answers. "Our men offered to take the
first watch and killed them as they slept, sir."

"Excellent work, Smee, now unlock the door," Captain Hook
orders.

"Aye, Captain," Smee responds. He fumbles with the keys as
the second, far larger, guard slides the cell door open.

"Your father" Admiral Price chokes out, "wasn't my fault." At
that, his eyes darken and he is gone.

Captain Hook rifles through the admiral's pockets and
retrieves the watch. He bounds to the stairs and climbs onto the main
deck. What he finds on the deck is no less than he expects. All of his
men, the entire crew of the *Jolly Roger*, stand cheering in their Royal
Navy uniforms. Even the deafening waves of the killing sea couldn't

drown out their hearty celebration.

Captain Hook checks the time, looks to the clearing sky and the first stars of this night, and nods his approval. The last pattering of rain taps the deck softly. Soon, it too is gone.

"Ready to cast off, Captain," Smee calls out from the deck. "What should we do with the *Triumph*?"

"What else? Raid it. Burn it," Captain Hook says to uproarious applause.

"I believe these are yours, Captain." The large crewman hands him the three gold coins.

"Thank you, Mr. Jukes," Hook says. He studies the coins for a long moment before dropping them over the bow and into the ocean depths forever. "Today, William, we avenged our fathers' deaths. Our long journey is at an end at last." Yet even as Captain Hook says these words, he could not begin to imagine how wrong he is.

Chapter Thirty-Seven

Captain James Hook strides on the deck of the *Jolly Roger*. Her tall masts cut a frightening silhouette into the sky. Hook looks over his shoulder at Admiral Price's flagship, the *Triumph*, as it burns.

"Bring me Long Tom," he orders. Cheers roar from the crew as three men roll the ship-killer into position. They load and pack the cannon. Captain Hook aims and lights the fuse. Thunder sounds and boards fly from the once proud flagship. It sinks slowly, but James Hook insists on watching every instant of it.

"It's over," he says to himself. He believes it to be true. In the names of all who were lost, his father, his mother, Mr. Jukes, and especially Emily, all who were responsible were punished. Heath Ashley is dead. Jesse Labette is dead. Admiral Price is dead. Everyone who was at fault.

Fault.

The word plays over in James Hook's head as if he should

know the hidden meaning behind it. He remembers Admiral Price's dying words, *Your father wasn't my fault.* He had heard that before, when Emily said it about Heath Ashley, *It's not his fault.* Up until now he thought that she was referring to the gunshot that killed her, but he begins to put the puzzle together.

The charts. There was another set of lines on those charts. Those were for the ship belonging to Captain Ashley. He was to rendezvous with his father's ship to capture Jesse Labette as a fleet. Until now, he thought that Ashley was late.

Captain Hook's heart sinks as waves of realization crash against him. He changed the charts and made his father's ship arrive early. His footing gives way and he grasps the railing to prevent from falling over. One terrible thought burns in his mind: he brought his father to his death.

Hook grips the railing hard and rights himself as another thought enters his mind. He wasn't alone. Peter Pan was with him. Hook stops and does the quick math in his head. His room. This ship. The charts. The island. *The fault,* Captain Hook thinks, *belongs squarely on Pan's shoulders. Of those who wronged my father, only Peter Pan remains.* There's joy in this revelation. It's the kind of joy that one finds when solving a riddle which has long eluded them. It's the kind of joy that Hook hasn't allowed himself to feel for years.

At that moment, a faint glimmer of light catches Captain Hook's eye. He knows what it is before he sees it fully. He wishes he could deny it exists, but he knows better. The light dances just beyond reach as the crew looks on in stunned amazement. Hook lashes out for her, but she dodges, spilling a faint trail of fairy dust with each quick movement.

"I see your fairy, Peter Pan," Captain Hook calls out. "Where Tinkerbell is, you aren't far behind. Show yourself!" Two barrels tumble over and a flash of green rushes by Captain Hook's head with a familiar, infuriating giggle. Hook draws his sword but cuts only air. James falls to the deck as Peter Pan weaves between the sails of the *Jolly Roger* and hangs on the mast. Hardened sailors stare in childlike wonder at the magical boy in green.

"I'm Peter Pan," the boy says through a proud smile. Pan smiles and waves at the practiced killers, who are now stunned with awe. The boy floats down off of the mast and hovers inches from the floorboards.

Captain Hook rises from the deck of the *Jolly Roger* to meet Peter Pan eye to eye.

"Where did you come from?" Hook asks. Peter looks curiously at the strange man and his odd greeting

"I was here the whole time," Peter says. "I heard the battle from the island and came over to watch." Captain Hook's heart jumps into his throat at the mention of the island. He looks from side to side, until, at last, he sees land in the distance. He rushes over to the starboard railing and sees the same island he washed up on years ago. Bill Jukes drops his sword and walks up by his side.

"The storm must have blown us here," Jukes says.

"Perhaps," Hook says.

Peter dances on the breeze that carries him over to the railing as well. "I saw this ship and wanted to play," he says. "I don't have toys this nice where I'm from."

"You know this ship," Hook says. "You've been here before." Pan looks on in vacant doubt as Captain Hook stretches his arm out towards his cabin. "That night, you ducked into my father's quarters. I followed you and changed the course my father plotted, but if it wasn't for you, I wouldn't have been tempted into his cabin in the first place."

Peter, unsure of what to make of this strange man's words, cocks his head to the side. He stares questioningly at the crewmen, who, in return, are frozen in amazement and offer Pan no help in understanding what is going on.

"Point in fact," Hook continues, "it was my telling of you to my parents that got me put on this ship in the first place." In an instant, the intended life of James Hoodkins unfolds before Captain Hook's eyes. If not for Peter Pan, his father and mother would have lived to see him become a scholar at Eton. He would have had a quiet life in London with Emily by his side. There would be children, grandchildren, and holiday dinners. None of that is to happen now.

Peter, increasingly certain that there is no fun to be found here, carries himself towards the stars until, quite unexpectedly, a hand clasps his ankle.

"Oh, no you don't," Hook says.

"Let go of me!" Peter shouts.

"Not until you learn that there are consequences for your actions," Hook says. Peter looks down into Hook's eyes and smiles. With his free foot, Pan kicks himself free. He loops in the air and draws his short sword.

"Let's play pirates," Pan says. "What a game that would be!"

"You've said that before, as well," Hook says.

"I did?"

"It was on this ship, back when I told you of Jesse Labette."

"Wow," Peter says. "And now you're here." He pauses for a moment and puffs his chest. "I'm so clever."

"Indeed you are, boy," Hook says. "Seize him!" All but Bill Jukes hesitate a second too long. Even so, he misses Peter by a hair. One by one, the men grasp for the boy only to tumble over each other stupidly.

"You'll never catch me," Pan says.

"Of course not," Hook admits. "You've made fools of men for far too long."

Captain Hook starts sending the pirates at Peter in calculated waves. Peter gracefully ducks and dodges the men, but is unwittingly drawn closer to the center of the ship with each pass. He circles around several times, until finally, Peter is met with the tip of Captain Hook's sword. Pan parries with his sword and turns to counter.

Captain Hook is there to meet him. Steel clashes as the two begin exchanging attacks.

"Tell me again about the children you take in the night," Hook says. He slashes at the air where Peter once stood. "Tell me about Donald Sotheby."

"Who?" Peter asks, jabbing at Hook and catching nothing.

"Curly," Hook says. He thrusts twice before looking into Pan's clueless eyes. "The Lost Boys!" he shouts. "Do they mean nothing to you?"

"The Lost Boys are great!" Peter says. Pan blocks two more swipes before adding, "as long as they do as I say and don't get too old."

"And if they do grow too old or disobey you?" Hook asks. Pan pushes away from Captain Hook and pauses for a moment before answering.

"I thin them out," he says. It is such a curious answer that Hook can't resist probing further.

"Thin them out?"

"Some go back."

"After how long?" Hook asks. "Years? Decades? Do they even recognize the world you return them to?" Hook seethes for several seconds before collecting his thoughts. But when his mind clears, one question pushes its way forward. "You said that some go back. What about the others?"

"They get killed," Pan says. "Like this." Peter makes several short stabbing motions in the air.

Captain Hook will admit to a great many evil deeds, not the least of which is murder, theft, and piracy. But the sight of Peter Pan calmly describing the slaying of his own Lost Boys chills him to his core.

"I will end you, Peter Pan." With his left hand, the pirate draws a boarding hook from within his coat. Captain Hook attacks and Peter rushes to meet him. Hook slashes crossways and thrusts low. Pan darts left and tries to fly above, but is cut off. Hook thrusts and swipes high, forcing Peter closer to the deck. "You are through robbing parents of their families and robbing children of their futures."

"We play games," Peter says. Hook kicks two barrels out from under Peter's footing, forcing the boy to catch himself before falling.

"Enough with your games." Captain Hook slashes and swipes until finally the guard of his sword cracks against Peter's teeth. The crew watches, jaws agape, as the flying boy slams against the mast and slumps limply to the deck.

Captain Hook advances on the heap of skin and bone on his deck, his sword and hook at the ready for any attack. But when Pan sits himself upright and begins to sob at his bloodied face, Hook pauses.

Mother was right all those years ago, Hook realizes. *Peter Pan may command a sorcery that I don't yet understand, but no matter what evil or magic makes him act as he does, he's still just a boy, nothing more. Peter Pan can be hurt. Peter Pan can be killed.*

"You are a curse, Peter Pan," Hook says, drawing nearer. Peter is fully crying now, his hands covered with blood from his nose and teeth. Captain Hook draws still closer. "Your carelessness has ruined countless lives. Everything you touch turns to madness and that madness must end."

Captain Hook measures the distance and raises his blade for the killing blow. He shifts his weight, steps hard with the lead foot, and is met with a bright flash in his eyes. The sting sends his aim off. The sword drives hard into the mast, missing Peter by inches.

Tinkerbell rings loudly in Hook's ear. She stings him again and darts around behind him. Hook turns and swats her with the back of an open hand. She tumbles head over feet across the length of the ship, spilling fairy dust over Captain Hook and many of his crew.

Hook turns back to pull the sword from the mast. But as he grips it, Pan lifts himself up high, swings his sword down hard, and cleaves Hook's right hand off at the wrist.

James howls as thick blood oozes out onto the deck. Peter catches the hand before it falls and carries it over to the starboard railing. Filled with too much rage to be stopped by pain, James pulls his mother's old cloth off of the hilt of his father's sword and ties it taut on the wound to stop it from bleeding. He then straps the hook tight on the stump and chases after the boy. Peter smiles and tosses the hand overboard.

Hook rushes to the railing and reaches out for his hand, only to find the waiting jaws of the unnaturally large croc from the island. Hungry for revenge, she leaps from the water and snaps her jaws tightly around the severed hand. Her eyes ignite with enjoyment and she circles with anticipation for more. Hook jerks back in shock and his father's watch jostles free from his coat pocket. It twinkles in the light as it falls to the sea. Eager for another taste of Captain Hook's unusual blood, the croc swallows the watch whole as well.

"No!" James shouts. He pulls a pistol from Cecco's belt and fires it at the ancient beast. Shocked more by the sound than the wound, the croc swims away, ticking loudly, back to the island and her cave.

"Better learn to fight left-handed, Captain Hook," Pan says from high above. He hangs from the crow's nest, smiling and laughing through bloodied teeth. He then dips between the sails and takes off into the night's sky.

"Follow that boy!" Captain Hook shouts. In his heart there is the satisfaction of hunting the one boy, the one creature, most responsible for the suffering of an entire lifetime. The exhilaration in his chest ignites the spilled fairy dust. Sparkling gold light wraps around the ship, carrying it up and out of the water.

Captain James Hook points the *Jolly Roger* at the second star to the right and chases Peter Pan straight on 'till morning.

About the Authors

Jeremiah Kleckner is a teacher in Perth Amboy, New Jersey. When not grading papers or coaching wrestling, he enjoys singing, reading, writing, drawing, and spending time with his family.
www.JeremiahKleckner.com
Twitter: @J_Kleckner

Jeremy Marshall works at a private special needs school in New Jersey. Jeremy has always had a love of writing. In his spare time you can find him creating another story idea, riding his motorcycle, or spending time with his wife, Lori Marshall.

Acknowledgements

There were several people who helped make this book a possibility. We would like to thank our editors (in alphabetical order) Roy Marshall, Laurence Sanders, and Robert Shearer.

Vengeance doesn't rest...

Captain James Hook and The SIEGE of Neverland

Captain James Hook is lustful for vengeance—but how far is he prepared to go?

Consumed by a burning hatred, Hook will stop at nothing to enact his terrible revenge on his nemesis, Peter Pan. Arriving in Neverland, he finds himself in a hellish kingdom that obeys none of the laws of the universe.

Worse yet, Hook must stand against a terrible predator that no man can fight...

Continue the adventure at CaptainHookNovel.com today!

Made in the USA
Middletown, DE
19 June 2019